Disney's

# ATLANTIS
## THE LOST EMPIRE

Printed in the United States of America     May 2001

10  9  8  7  6  5  4  3  2  1

This book is set in 12-point Rockwell Light.

Library of Congress Card Catalog Number: 00-109826
ISBN: 0-7364-1086-4

www.randomhouse.com/kids/disney
www.disneybooks.com

# DISNEY'S
# ATLANTIS
## THE LOST EMPIRE

### THE JUNIOR NOVELIZATION

Adapted by Lara Bergen

Based upon the screenplay written by Tab Murphy

**Random House** 🏠 **New York**

# PROLOGUE

*B*oom! Boom! Boom! Ka-BOOOOM!

The earth trembled and quaked, and a mushroom cloud of smoke and flames filled the pale blue sky. Moments later, an armada of Atlantean stone fish vehicles flew away from the scene of the disaster.

*"NEE-puk!"* ("You fool!") shouted the lead pilot. *"GWEE-sit TEE-rid MEH-gid-lih-men!"* ("You've destroyed us all!")

The pilot raced over the open sea, and the rest of the armada sped along behind him. The vehicles glowed as their engines strained at their upper limit.

*"Shoam KOO-leh-beh-toat!"* ("It's gaining!") cried another frantic pilot. *"LOO-den-tem WEE-luhg KAH-behr-seh-kem!"* ("We have to warn the city!")

The armada raced toward its island home. These

were the greatest, most technologically advanced flying machines in the world. But they were no match for the giant wall of water rising from the ocean behind them—a deadly tidal wave the Atlanteans had created accidentally.

There was no way the armada would ever reach Atlantis safely.

*"Nahl YOH-deh-neh-toat!"* ("Too late!") the second pilot yelled as he felt the wave upon his tail. "AAAAAGHHHH!"

*"GWEE-sit khoab-DEH-sheh-toat!"* ("We're doomed!") *"SOH-lesh-tem MOO-tih-lihm-kem!"* ("All is lost!")

*"TEH-wuhn-toap! TEH-gu-len-tem gaom NOO-roash-yoakh!"* ("Everyone to the shelters!")

Loudspeaker warnings and alarms rang throughout the city of Atlantis. Lookouts had seen the enormous wave approaching. They knew there was no time to lose.

In the streets, other guards tried to keep the people calm.

*"WEH-shehk-mohl!"* ("Don't panic!")
*"Dihn-NOAKH!"* ("One at a time!")

But it was clear that there was reason to panic. Something was terribly wrong with the Crystal. Usually it hovered peacefully above the island, glowing a serene blue as it gave power to the city. But today the Atlanteans had used that power for evil, not for good. And today it was as if the Crystal were on fire!

Beams of red light shot out from its core. As the Atlanteans ran for cover, the beams darted this way and that, scouring the city like searchlights. The Crystal seemed to be looking for something—but what?

In the middle of it all stood the king and queen of Atlantis and their young daughter, Princess Kida.

*"Oat, TAH-nehb-taot. KEE-yihsh!"* their footman shouted. ("This way, Your Highness. Quickly!")

He tried to usher them through the crowd and into the royal shelter. Suddenly the tiny princess stopped and turned back the way they had come. She had dropped her doll.

*"KEE-duh-toap MAH-sihk!"* ("Kida, come on!") the queen called. She reached out and grabbed her daughter by the arm. *"TOH-kiht sehr KO-pehg! NAHL-tem WAH-nuh-teh-kem!"* ("Just leave it! There's no time!")

Tears welled in Kida's wide gray eyes as she looked up at her mother. The Crystal's ruby beam found the queen. She stopped, frozen in her tracks.

Kida watched as the beam turned from fiery red back to its usual blue and lifted her mother into the sky. For a moment, as she rose, the queen kept her hold on Kida's arm. But the Crystal's pull was too strong. At last, the queen's hand slipped away, clasping Kida's tiny gold bracelet.

*"MAH-tihm!"* ("Mother!") Kida cried as the queen floated up and into the bright blue Crystal. *"MAH-tihm!"*

But there was nothing she or the king could do.

As they looked on, a flurry of blue beams shot out from the Crystal's core. Quickly, the king gathered Kida into his arms and held her as the bright light formed a dome of pure, shimmering energy around Atlantis— and it was not a moment too soon! The massive tidal wave came crashing over the city!

*"OH-kweh-pen-tem MOH-khihn DEH-rem, KEE-duh-toap!"* ("Close your eyes, Kida!") he told her.

And the next thing Kida and the other Atlanteans knew, the wave had buried their shielded city beneath an ocean of salt water and foam.

# CHAPTER 1

## Washington, D.C., 1914
### (Five Thousand Years Later)

**I**nside a dimly lit room in a world-famous museum, Milo Thatch looked up eagerly from his podium and addressed the silent audience before him.

"Good afternoon, gentlemen," he said, straightening his bow tie. "First off, I'd like to thank this board for taking the time to hear my proposal."

Then, clearing his throat, he indicated with his pointer the big blue area of a map drawn on the chalkboard behind him.

"Now, we've all heard the legend of Atlantis—of a continent somewhere in the mid-Atlantic that was home to an advanced civilization, possessing technology far beyond our own . . ."

Milo paused to point at a marble bust.

". . . that, according to our friend Plato here,

was suddenly struck by some cataclysmic event that sank it beneath the sea. Now, some of you may ask, 'Why Atlantis? It's just a myth, isn't it? Pure fantasy.' Well, that is where you'd be wrong!"

Milo's eyes twinkled behind his thick round glasses as he went on.

"Ten thousand years before the Egyptians built the pyramids, Atlantis had electricity, advanced medicine, even the power of *flight*! Impossible, you say?" He grinned and shook his head at his speechless audience. "Numerous ancient cultures all over the globe agree that Atlantis possessed a power source of some kind, more powerful than steam, coal, and even our modern internal combustion engines."

Milo took a deep breath.

"Gentlemen, I propose that we find Atlantis, find that power source, and bring it back to the surface!"

To illustrate his point, Milo held up a page from an ancient book.

"This is a page from an illuminated text that describes a book called *The Shepherd's Journal*. It is said to have been a firsthand account of Atlantis and its exact whereabouts. Now, based on a centuries-old translation of a Norse text, historians have believed the Journal resides in Ireland."

Milo let out a grunt as he lifted a heavy iron shield.

"But," he went on, pushing his glasses back into place, "after comparing the text to the runes on this Viking shield, I found that one of the letters had been mistranslated."

He pointed to a symbol near the bottom of the shield.

"So, by changing this letter and inserting the correct one, we find that *The Shepherd's Journal,* the key to Atlantis, lies *not* in Ireland, gentlemen, but in *Iceland*.

"Pause for effect . . . ," Milo murmured under his breath.

Then he looked out over his audience with a self-satisfied grin. "Gentlemen, I'll take your questions now."

*Brrrringgg! Brrrringgg!*

Milo jumped. The telephone!

"Uh, would you gentlemen please excuse me for a moment?" he muttered.

He turned, climbed onto the swiveling chalkboard behind him, and pushed the board over, landing squarely on top of his desk on the other side.

"Cartography and Linguistics," he answered breathlessly. "Milo Thatch speaking!"

He cringed as a shrill voice screeched in his ear.

"Yeah, yeah. Just a second," he muttered.

Frowning, he flipped a light switch on the wall. Instantly, the dim "boardroom" was bathed in light. And if there had been anyone else in the room—the *boiler* room—they would have seen that Milo's "audience" was nothing more than a collection of skeletons and statues wearing African masks and top hats.

"Pardon me, Mr. Hickenbottom," Milo said as he inched past a skeleton to get to the boiler.

He turned a few knobs, whacked the furnace with a wrench, then walked back to the phone.

"How's that?" he said into the mouthpiece. "Is that better? You're welcome. Uh, bye."

Milo hung up the phone and turned back to his silent audience.

"As you can see by this map that I've drawn, I've plotted the route that will take myself and a crew to the southern coast of Iceland to retrieve the Journal—"

*Cuc-koo. Cuc-koo. Cuc-koo. Cuc-koo.*

"Ah, showtime!" exclaimed Milo, glancing up at the striking clock on the wall. "Well, this is it. I'm finally getting out of the dungeon!" He picked up his maps and papers and headed out of the room.

On the way, he stopped at a sort of small shrine near the door and carefully opened it. Inside was a well-worn explorer's pith helmet and a small framed photograph of an old man and a child.

Looking at the picture, Milo could almost feel Grandpa Thatch placing the helmet on his young head. He couldn't have been more than six or seven years old at the time, but he remembered it as if it were yesterday.

*Shhthunk!*

At that moment, a message came whooshing into the pneumatic tube next to the door.

Milo opened the message container, unrolled the paper, and read:

```
Dear Mr. Thatch:
This is to inform you that
your meeting today has been
moved up from 4:30 p.m.
to 3:30 p.m.
Mr. Harcourt's Office
```

"What!" exclaimed Milo. He looked frantically up at the clock. It was already four o'clock!

*Shhthunk!*

A second message arrived.

```
Dear Mr. Thatch:

Due to your absence, the
board has voted to reject
your proposal. Have a nice
weekend.

Mr. Harcourt's Office
```

"They can't do this to me!" Milo shouted.

He grabbed his coat and papers and hurried out the door.

By the time he reached the conference room on the main floor, the stuffy members of the museum's board of directors were waddling away.

"I swear, that young Thatch gets crazier every year," one muttered.

"If I ever hear the word 'Atlantis' again, I'll step in

front of a bus," said another.

"Ha, ha, ha! I'll push you," laughed a third.

"Mr. Harcourt!" Milo called from across the hall. He smiled and waved at the chairman of the board.

"Good Lord!" one of the men shouted. "There he is!"

The pudgy old men fell over themselves in a desperate attempt to avoid Milo.

"How did you find us?" cried Mr. Harcourt as he tried to push past his colleagues. "Get away! Where is a guard when you need him?"

"Mr. Harcourt, wait!" Milo pleaded. "You gotta listen to me, sir!"

He followed the chairman through the museum and out the front door.

"Sir, I—I have new evidence that . . . ," Milo stammered.

But it was no use. Harcourt climbed into his waiting car and his chauffeur closed the door. Only then did the old gentleman turn to address Milo through the open car window.

"This museum funds scientific expeditions based on *facts*, not legends and folklore," he told Milo. "Besides, we need you *here*. We *depend* on you."

"You do?" Milo asked, surprised.

Harcourt nodded. "Yes! What with winter coming, that boiler's going to need a lot of attention."

"Boiler?" Milo stood stunned for a moment as the chairman's car rumbled off. Then he began to chase it.

"Sir," he cried as he leaped onto the hood of the moving car, "I really hoped it wouldn't come to this." He struggled to pull a piece of paper out of his coat pocket. "But this is a letter of resignation. If you reject my proposal, I'll . . . WHOA!"

The big car swerved. And the next thing Milo knew—*SPLAT*—he and his letter were lying, soaked, in the gutter.

"I'll quit!" he yelled after the car. He was pleased and a little surprised to see the car stop and back up.

"I mean it, sir," Milo said as the car rolled up beside him. "If you refuse to fund my proposal . . ."

"You'll what?" Harcourt asked, leaning out the window. "Flush your career down the toilet just like your grandfather? You have a lot of potential, Milo. Don't throw it all away chasing fairy tales."

"But I can *prove* Atlantis exists!" Milo declared.

The old man just rolled his eyes. "You want to go on an expedition? Here!" He tossed a coin at Milo's feet.

"Take a trolley to the Potomac and jump in. Maybe the cold water will clear your head!"

With a loud screech, the black car sped off, showering Milo with dirty water.

Milo swallowed hard as he tried to wipe the mud off his glasses. What was he going to do? How would he ever find Atlantis now?

He looked over at his maps and papers, scattered along the curb. *At least they're still dry,* he thought.

Then it started to rain.

# CHAPTER 2

**"I**'m home! Fluffy?" Milo called as he opened the door to his apartment. "Here, kitty."

He reached out to flip on the light. But no light came on. *Click, click, click.* He tried the switch a few more times.

"Milo James Thatch?"

Milo jumped at the sound of a voice from across the room. Lightning from the storm outside illuminated the speaker.

"What? Who are you?" he said to the beautiful stranger sitting in a chair by the window. His eyes traveled from her blond hair to her bare shoulders and down to her high-heeled shoes. "How'd you get in here?"

The mysterious woman smiled.

"I came down the chimney. Ho, ho, ho."

She crossed her long legs and stared at Milo.

"My name is Helga Sinclair. I'm acting on behalf of my employer, who has a most intriguing proposition for you. Are you interested?"

Milo was speechless for a moment.

"Your employer?" he finally asked. "Who is your employer?"

"Step lively," Helga told Milo. "Mr. Whitmore does not like to be kept waiting."

Milo soon found himself inside the largest, grandest mansion he'd ever seen. As he followed his mysterious guide down a wide hallway, he marveled at the countless treasures lining the walls.

She led him into an elevator at the end of the hall. As the elevator descended, she turned and gave him a thorough inspection.

"You will address him as 'Mr. Whitmore' or 'sir,'" she instructed as she straightened Milo's tie. "You will stand unless asked to be seated. Keep your sentences short and to the point." She squinted at him through her long, curved lashes. "Are we clear?"

Milo nodded nervously. The elevator doors slid open

and he stepped out into another huge, treasure-filled room. Helga remained in the elevator.

"And relax," she added as the doors slid shut. "He doesn't bite . . . often."

Milo took a hesitant step forward. Then another. And another. In all his years at the museum, he had never seen so many priceless objects together in one room. Marble statues. Silk rugs. Gold and silver suits of armor. Carvings from Africa and altars from the Far East. He didn't know where to look first.

Then a life-size portrait on the wall caught his eye, and he stopped and stared.

"Grandpa?" he said with a gasp.

"Finest explorer I ever met," a voice declared.

Milo's head whipped around . . . and down to a pretzel-shaped figure on the floor. Milo took a closer look. It was an old man in a tunic.

"Preston Whitmore," the man announced. Cheerfully, he offered his wrinkled bare foot for Milo to shake. "It's a pleasure to meet you, Milo. Join me in a little yoga?"

Then he took his head in his hands and shifted his neck from side to side—*crrickk, crrackk.*

Milo looked down at him, bewildered. "N-no, thank

you," he stammered as he gave the man's foot a polite little shake. "Did you really know my grandfather?"

*Crrrraaaack! Crrriiiick! Pop!*

Mr. Whitmore continued to stretch and crack his joints one by one.

"Oh, yeah, met old Thaddeus back in Georgetown. Class of 1866. We stayed close friends till the end of his days . . . even dragged me along on some of his dang fool expeditions. Thatch was crazy as a fruit bat, he was. He spoke of you often."

"Funny," Milo said. "He never mentioned you."

Whitmore smoothed his snow-white beard. "Oh, he wouldn't," he said. "He knew how much I like my privacy." And with that, the old man leaned over and stood on his head.

"Y'know," Whitmore went on cheerfully, "some people say I'm eccentric. Ahhh . . . ," he sighed as he stretched. "Well, call it what you want. I keep a low profile."

Milo nodded and waited awkwardly for Whitmore to turn upright. At last Milo got down on his knees to speak to his upside-down host face to face.

"Uh, Mr. Whitmore, should I be wondering why I am here?" he asked.

Still standing on his head, the old man pointed to a table across the room. "Look on that table," he told Milo. "It's for you."

The package sitting on the table was clearly labeled "Milo Thatch." Milo recognized the handwriting right away.

"It's from my grandfather," he said with a gasp.

Behind him, Mr. Whitmore had moved on from yoga to tai chi. He now stood on one foot, waving his arms in wide, slow circles.

"He brought that package to me years ago," Whitmore explained. "He said if anything were to happen to him I should give it to you when you were ready . . . whatever that means."

Breathless, Milo peeled back the stiff brown paper to reveal an ancient book. He traced his finger over a large symbol stamped into the cover.

"It can't be!" Milo exclaimed as a shiver ran down his spine. "It's *The Shepherd's Journal*!"

Whitmore walked up behind Milo and peered over his shoulder.

"Mr. Whitmore," Milo went on, "this journal is the key to finding the lost continent of Atlantis!"

"Atlantis?" the old man replied. He shook his head

and patted Milo good-naturedly on the shoulder. "I wasn't born yesterday, son."

"No, look," Milo said as he flipped through the yellowed pages. Each one was filled with ancient drawings and symbols. "Look at this—coordinates, clues," he said. "It's all right here."

Whitmore frowned and stepped behind a screen to change out of his yoga clothes. "Looks like gibberish to me," he scoffed.

"That's because it's been written in a dialect that no longer exists," Milo explained.

"So it's useless," quipped the old man. He tossed his tunic over the screen.

"No, no!" Milo replied excitedly. "Just difficult. I've spent my whole life studying dead languages. It's not gibberish to me."

Mr. Whitmore came out from behind the screen dressed in a fancy suit and holding a silver-tipped cane.

"Ah," he said, rubbing his beard thoughtfully, "it's probably a fake."

Milo snapped the book shut, exasperated.

"Mr. Whitmore," he said, "my grandfather would have known if this were a fake. *I* would know." He held up the Journal and waved it in front of the old man's face. "I will stake everything I own, everything I believe in, that this is the genuine *Shepherd's Journal*!"

Whitmore took a deep breath, then slowly turned away. He walked to an armchair by the fireplace and sat down. "All right, all right," he said. "So what do you want to do with it?"

Milo raised his eyebrows. He didn't know what to say. "Well, I'll, I'll, I'll get funding. I mean . . . I'll . . . the museum will . . ."

"They'll never believe you," said Whitmore.

"I'll show them!" Milo declared with a pump of his fist. "I will make them believe!"

Now it was Whitmore's turn to raise his eyebrows. "Like you did today?"

Milo stopped in his tracks and his mouth fell open. "Yes! No! How did you know?" Then he waved the whole idea of the museum away. "Forget about them, okay? Never mind. I will find Atlantis on my own! Even if I have to rent a rowboat!"

Mr. Whitmore eyed Milo thoughtfully and was silent for a moment. Suddenly, his face broke into a huge, sunny smile.

"Congratulations, Milo," he said. "This is exactly what

I wanted to hear. But forget the rowboat, son. We'll travel in style!"

The billionaire pushed a button, and the next thing Milo knew, a row of miniature model vehicles automatically rose out of the table at Whitmore's side. There were ships and trucks and airplanes, a hot-air balloon and a submarine—every type of expedition vehicle Milo could imagine.

"It's all been arranged," Mr. Whitmore went on as he picked up one of the models. "The whole ball of wax!"

"Why?" Milo asked, utterly befuddled.

The old man chuckled. "For years your granddad bent my ear with stories about that old book," he told Milo, pointing at the Journal. "I didn't buy it for a minute. So, finally I got fed up, and I made a bet with the ol' coot. I said, 'Thatch, if you ever actually find that so-called Journal, not only will I finance the expedition, but I'll kiss ya full on the mouth." Whitmore grinned. "Imagine my embarrassment when he found the darn thing."

Then his wrinkled face became serious.

"Your grandpa was a great man," Whitmore told Milo. "Those buffoons at the museum dragged him down and made a laughingstock of him. He died a broken man. If I could bring back just one shred of proof, that would be enough for me."

Whitmore sighed a heavy sigh. "Ah, Thatch." Then he looked at Milo. "Well, what're we standin' around for? We've got work to do!"

"But, Mr. Whitmore," Milo said meekly, "in order to do what you're proposing, you're gonna need a crew."

"Taken care of!" announced Whitmore. Proudly, he pulled out a stack of dossiers and spread them on the table. He held up a picture of Milo's grandfather holding *The Shepherd's Journal* with a happy crew around him. "The best of the best," Whitmore said, pointing to each one. "Gaetan Molière. Geologist and excavator. Man has a nose for dirt. Vincenzo Santorini. Demolitions. Busted him out of a Turkish prison. And Audrey Ramirez. Don't let her age fool you. She's forgotten more about engines than you and I will ever know." Milo counted three or four more crew members in the photo. "They're the same crew that brought the Journal back," Whitmore added.

"Where was it?" Milo asked, his curiosity piqued.

"Iceland."

"I knew it, I knew it!" Milo slapped his knee.

"All we need now is an expert in gibberish," said Mr. Whitmore, looking meaningfully at Milo. "So . . . it's decision time."

Milo jumped up as he tried to take it all in. "I'll—I'll have to quit my job."

"It's done," Whitmore said. "You resigned this afternoon."

"I did?" Milo gulped.

"Yep."

"My apartment . . . I'm going to have to give notice."

"Taken care of."

"My clothes?"

"Packed."

"My books?"

"In storage."

"My cat?"

*Meow.* Fluffy jumped onto his shoulder.

Milo gulped. This was all so sudden. In one way, it was like a dream come true. But in another way, it was terrifying. He didn't know what to say—or what to do.

Mr. Whitmore reached out and placed his hand on Milo's shoulder. "Your granddad had a saying," he told Milo, looking into his eyes. "'Our lives are remembered by the gifts we leave our children.' This Journal is his gift to you, Milo. Atlantis is waiting. What do you say?"

Milo looked down at the weathered Journal. Over the last thousand years, it had gone around the world. And now—thanks to Grandpa Thatch—it had landed in his lap.

He looked at the billionaire and smiled.

"I'm your man, Mr. Whitmore!"

# CHAPTER 3

**M**ilo felt as if he were caught in a whirlwind. Before he knew it, he and his crewmates were on board a steamship bound for Atlantis. Mr. Whitmore had taken care of all the logistical details. Now Milo just had to overcome one small problem—seasickness.

Queasily, he left the ship's deck and the railing he'd been clutching for an hour and made his way inside the ship and through an enormous garage. Around him stood vehicles of every shape and size—enormous, strange-looking machines—with hundreds of mechanics tweaking this and tightening that.

Milo walked up to an official-looking woman in a military uniform and tapped her on the back. "Excuse me?" he said. "I need to report in."

The woman turned to face him—and pushed back a strand of long blond hair.

"Yes, Mr. Thatch?" said Helga.

"Ah!" Milo gasped. "It's you!"

Meanwhile, a clunky, overloaded covered wagon was being lowered by a crane onto the loading bay behind them.

"Blondie!" called a long-whiskered old-timer from the front seat. "I got a bone to pick with you!"

"Hold that thought," Helga told Milo. Then she turned to the crotchety wagon driver. "What is it this time, Cookie?" she asked.

"You done stuffed my wagon full to bustin' with nonessentials," he complained. He rummaged through a crate and held up a few items to show her. "Lookit all this! Cinnamon? Oregano? Cilantro! What in the cockadoodle is cilantro?"

Then, still grumbling, he reached into another box. "What is this?"

"That would be lettuce," Helga replied in her usual no-nonsense tone.

"Lettuce? Lettuce!" Cookie looked disgusted and confused.

"It's a vegetable, Cookie," Helga explained. "The men need the four basic food groups."

"I got your four basic food groups," Cookie scoffed. "Beans, bacon, whiskey, and lard!"

*Weee-ahhhh! Weee-ahhhh!*

Milo jumped at the loud wail of a siren.

Helga marked something on her clipboard and gave Cookie a commanding nod. "All right, cowboy," she said brusquely, "pack it up and move it out!"

A gravelly, monotonous woman's voice boomed over the loudspeaker. "Attention. All hands to launch bay. Final loading in progress."

Milo looked around him. Crew members were starting to run this way and that. Machines were being pushed and pulled. And everything was moving toward one enormous vessel—the *Ulysses*—a state-of-the-art, one-of-a-kind submarine that would be launched from the ship to carry the explorers on their underwater journey.

"Wow!" Milo exclaimed.

"Hey, Junior," called a gruff voice with a heavy Italian accent, "if you're looking for the pony rides, they're back there."

Milo jumped back as a man with a big black mustache brushed by, rolling a heavy barrel.

"Excuse me . . . excuse me?" Milo called to him. He reached down and picked up a thick red stick that had fallen to the ground. "You dropped your dy—*dynamite*! What else have you got in there?"

The man—Vinny Santorini, demolitions expert—stopped and poked casually through his load. "Oh, gunpowder, nitroglycerin, notepads, fuses, wicks, glue, uh, paper clips—big ones." He shrugged. "You know, just office supplies."

Milo shrank away from the barrel of explosives, slowly and without making any sudden moves. Then a familiar voice made him turn around.

"Milo! Where ya been?" Preston Whitmore shouted from the loading platform. He patted the arm of a tall, rugged man in uniform who stood beside him. "I want you to meet Commander Rourke. He led the Iceland team that brought the Journal back."

Commander Rourke extended a thick, muscular hand and gave Milo an arm-numbing shake. "Milo Thatch," he said with a tight smile. "Pleasure to meet the grandson of ol' Thaddeus. See you got that Journal. Nice pictures, but I prefer a good Western myself."

Mr. Whitmore's blue eyes twinkled as he surveyed the busy loading operation. "Pretty impressive, eh?" he said, motioning toward the vehicle convoy being loaded onto the submarine.

Milo grinned in admiration. "Boy, when you settle a bet, you settle a bet."

"Well, your granddad always believed you couldn't put a price on the pursuit of knowledge."

Milo nodded. "Yeah . . . believe me," he said. "This'll be small change compared to the value of what we'll learn on this trip."

Commander Rourke slowly rubbed his hands together. "Yes," he said. "This should be enriching for all of us."

"Attention, all personnel," the monotonous loudspeaker voice called out once again. "Launch will commence in fifteen minutes."

Whitmore turned to embrace Milo. Then Milo started up the gangplank.

"Make us proud, boy!" Mr. Whitmore shouted as Milo waved good-bye.

While Commander Rourke and his officers steered the submarine into the ocean depths, Milo wandered through the narrow hallways of the sub until he found his cabin.

*"Ahhh-mmm,"* he said, yawning and stretching.

He tossed his gear to the floor and jumped onto the bottom bunk. Not exactly a feather bed, he thought as he lay back on the thin mattress. But it would have to do.

"You have disturbed the dirt!"

Suddenly a panicked voice with a French accent made his eyes pop open.

"Ah, pardon me?" Milo said groggily. All he could see was a tiny light shining down from the bunk above him. But the smell . . . *that* was everywhere. Milo's hand flew up to his nose.

"You have disturbed the dirt!" the voice repeated.

After a few moments, Milo could just make out a buck-toothed face beneath the tiny headlight. The owner of the face had thick goggle-like glasses and a heavy five-o'clock shadow. And he was obviously very, very angry.

With a low growl, he jumped down onto Milo's bunk and yanked back the sheets. Sure enough, there on the mattress were small mounds of dirt—each marked with a flag from a different country.

"Dirt from around the globe! Spanning the centuries!

What have you done?" Lovingly, the little man picked up a tiny grain of dirt and moved it from one mound to another. "England must never merge with France!"

"What's it doing in my bed?" Milo asked.

The little man glared at Milo through his bulging goggles. "You ask too many questions! Who are you? Who sent you? Speak up!"

"Me?" said Milo. "I'm—"

"Bah! I will know soon enough!" spat the man.

With that, he grabbed Milo's hand and, squinting, inspected his fingernails.

"Hey, hey, hey—let go!" Milo cried. He didn't like having his hand held by someone who clearly never washed his own.

"Do not be such a crybaby! Hold still!"

Then Gaetan "Mole" Molière whipped a pair of tweezers out of his pocket and pried a tiny speck of dirt out from under Milo's nail.

"Aha!" he exclaimed, holding the dirt in front of his nose. "There you are! Now tell me your story, my little friend." He reached up to his goggles and extended his eyepiece to get a close look at the specimen. "Lead from the pencil," he mused. "You chew the eraser. Ham sandwich, no mayo. I see you have a cat. Mold spores from Mesopotamian parchment circa 2000 B.C. These are all the microscopic fingerprints of the mapmaker."

Then Mole stuck out his tongue and gave the dirt a little taste. *"Phfft,"* he spat with disgust, "and *linguist.*"

Milo was amazed. "Hey, how did—"

But Milo's duffel bag was tossed in his face before he could get another word out.

"This is an outrage!" Mole shrieked as he pushed Milo out the door. "You must leave at once! Out! Out! Out! Out! Out!"

Overcome by Mole's intensity, and by his powerful odor, Milo stumbled backward into the hallway—and right into a crewmate on his way to the shower.

"Uh-oh. Sat in that dirt, didn't you?" the tall, dark-skinned man said knowingly. "Mole! Now, what have I told you about playing nice with the other kids?" He stepped into the cabin and held out his bar of soap at Mole as if warding off a vampire. Milo cautiously tagged along behind him.

Mole cringed at the sight of the waxy white bar. "No!" he said in horror.

"Get back!" the man went on. "I've got soap and I'm not afraid to use it! Back, foul creature! Back to the pit from whence you came!"

He chuckled as Mole scrambled back onto his bunk and hid under the covers. Then the man turned to Milo and smiled.

"Name's Sweet," he said, offering a large, warm hand. "Joshua Sweet. Medical officer."

"Milo Thatch," said Milo.

"Milo Thatch! You're my three o'clock! Well—no time like the present." He rummaged through his medical bag and pulled out a large saw.

"Oh, boy." Milo gulped. He took a nervous step back.

Dr. Sweet grinned. "Nice, isn't it?" He held up the blade so that it gleamed in the bright fluorescent light. "The catalog says this little beauty can saw through a femur in twenty-eight seconds. I'm betting I can cut that time in half. Now, stick out your tongue and say 'ahh.'"

With relief, Milo watched Sweet stick the saw back into his bag and pull out a thermometer.

"So, where ya from?" the doctor asked as he jammed the instrument into Milo's mouth.

*"Iggle! Iggle! Algaee!"*

"Really?" said Sweet. "I have family up that way. Beautiful country up there. Ya do any fishing?"

*"Mmp! Miggle mump!"*

The doctor shook his head. "Me? I hate fishing. I hate

fish. Hate the taste, hate the smell, and hate all them little bones."

Sweet was still shaking his head as he walked away—only to return seconds later with two very large glass jars.

"Here. I'm gonna need you to fill these up," he explained as he handed them to Milo.

*"Ssspluhh!"* The thermometer went flying. "With what?" Milo cried.

Just then, the familiar emotionless voice came blaring through the speakers. "Will Mr. Thatch please report to the bridge?"

"Thank you." Milo closed his eyes and sighed. Then he looked up at the eager doctor. "I mean, nice meeting you."

Sweet cradled his jars and nodded. "Nice meeting you, too."

# CHAPTER 4

After a few wrong turns, Milo found his way to the sub's control deck. It was a very busy place—full of busy men and women working the controls. And in the middle of them all was a very busy Commander Rourke.

He looked up from his periscope as Milo walked in, and waved.

"Welcome to the bridge, Mr. Thatch," he called. "Okay, everybody, I want you to give Mr. Thatch your undivided attention."

As Milo took his place in front of a large white screen, he noticed the chief members of the expedition crew settling into a row of chairs facing him. A couple of them he had already met, including Helga, Vinny, and Mole. Milo recognized Audrey Ramirez, the expedition's chief mechanic, from Mr. Whitmore's dossier.

Nervously, he cleared his throat. "Good afternoon," he said. "Can everyone hear me okay?"

The audience stared back at him blankly.

"Okay . . . um, how about some slides? The first slide is a depiction of a creature. A creature so fightening that sailors were said to have been driven mad by the mere sight of it."

Milo pressed a button and the slide projector clicked. Up popped a picture of Milo posing in a bathing suit on a sandy beach.

"Whoo-hoo! Yow!" The crew whistled and howled.

Milo turned several shades of red as he fumbled with the projector button.

"Sorry," he mumbled. "That's wrong."

Eighteen-year-old Audrey groaned as she smacked her gum. "I used to take lunch money from guys like this."

"Anyway," Milo went on as another slide clicked into place. "This—" He checked the screen behind him. "Okay, this is an illustration of the Leviathan, the creature guarding the entrance to Atlantis."

To the crew, however, it looked more like a big, spiny lobster.

Vinny spoke up. "With something like that, I would have white wine, I think."

"It's a mythical sea serpent," Milo explained. "He's described in the Book of Job. The Bible says, 'Out of his mouth go burning lights, sparks of fire shoot out.' But more likely, it's a carving or a sculpture to frighten the superstitious."

Commander Rourke stood up to speak. "So we find this masterpiece. Then what?"

"When do we *dig*?" Mole shouted eagerly.

"Actually, we don't have to dig," Milo said, flashing another image onto the screen.

He pointed to a picture depicting the route to Atlantis.

"You see, according to the Journal, the path to Atlantis will take us down a tunnel at the bottom of the ocean. Then we'll come up a curve, into an air pocket, right here, where we'll find the remnants of an ancient highway that will lead us to Atlantis. Kind of like the grease trap in your sink."

"You said there would be digging," Mole complained to Rourke.

"Commander!" an officer at the controls suddenly called out. "You better come look at this, sir!"

Rourke stood up and addressed the crew before him. "Okay, class dismissed. Give me exterior lights."

The lights came on, illuminating the ocean floor. The crew could make out the wreckage of numerous ships strewn about the rocks.

"There are ships here from every era," Milo observed.

An older woman in earphones—the communications officer—called out to Rourke. "Commander. . ."

"Yes, Mrs. Packard, what is it?" Rourke replied.

She pointed to her headset. "I'm picking something up on the hydrophone that I think you should hear."

"Put it on speakers," Rourke commanded.

Suddenly, the sub was filled with an eerie screeching that echoed off the hard steel walls. Rourke's forehead knotted as he listened.

"What is it?" he asked. "A pod of whales?"

"Nah," Mrs. Packard answered. "Bigger."

"Sounds metallic," Helga said. "Could be an echo off one of the shipwrecks."

Milo slowly raised his hand.

"Is it just me," he said, "or is it getting louder?"

Sure enough, as the crew listened, the noise grew

louder and louder. Then, suddenly, it stopped.

"Well," said Helga, letting out a sigh. "Whatever it was, it's gone now."

"Helmsman," Rourke called out. "Bring us about. Tighten our search pattern and slow us to—"

*WHAMMM!*

The ship slammed to a stop. Milo and the others went flying across the bridge.

Milo landed in a corner. It felt as if the sub had hit something—something very large.

Then he saw it out the bridge window. It took his breath away: a huge, lobster-like creature—at least ten times larger than the submarine itself. Its enormous red eye glared fiercely at Milo.

To his horror, Milo realized this was the Leviathan. And it was no statue!

Rourke, however, was as cool as a sea cucumber. "Tell Cookie to melt the butter and bring out the bibs," he called out. "I want this lobster served up on a silver platter."

"Load the torpedo bays!" Helga ordered. "Subpod crew—battle stations!"

As Mole and Vinny and the other subpod pilots ran

to their fighters, Milo felt another lurch and heard the squeal of twisting metal. He peered out the window once again and his jaw dropped.

"Jiminy Christmas!" he cried. The Leviathan's powerful claws were squeezing the sub like a tube of toothpaste. Through the large window on the bridge, Milo stared out at the monster's giant red eye. Only, it seemed to operate more like a mechanical shutter than the eye of a living creature. "It's a machine!"

*CRRAAACKK! P-P-POPPP!*

Slowly but surely, their indestructible sub was being crushed!

"Launch subpods!" Rourke ordered.

"Subpods away!"

One by one, the smaller ships shot out from the sub's launching docks. They quickly surrounded the Leviathan and attacked the metal beast. After one round of torpedoes, the Leviathan released its grip.

"We're free!" Rourke shouted from the bridge. "All ahead full!"

Meanwhile, down in the boiler room, things were getting messy. Audrey was doing everything she could to hold the engines together. But it was a losing battle. Bolts were popping, seams were cracking, and water was spraying everywhere.

"Get me the bridge!" she yelled to her engineering crew.

Up in the control room, Milo and the others could hear the panic in Audrey's voice as she yelled over the intercom.

"Rourke!" she barked. "We took a big hit down here, and we're taking on water fast. I don't want to be around when it hits the boiler."

"How much time do we have?" Rourke asked.

"Twenty minutes if the bulkhead holds."

*BOOOOOM!*

"You better make that five," Audrey added.

"You heard the lady," Rourke said, turning to his crew. "Let's move!"

Milo looked around, bewildered, as all the other crew members ran past him. "Move?" he said. "Where? Move where?"

Helga hurried over to the communications bay. "Packard," she said, "sound the alarm!"

Mrs. Packard, however, was deep in conversation with a friend back home. "He took his suitcase? Marge, honey, I don't think he's coming back."

"Packard!" Helga yelled.

The communications officer rolled her eyes. "I have to call you back," she said into her microphone. "No, no, I'll call you." Then she flipped the channel on her radio headset. "All hands abandon ship," she announced in her bored voice. "All hands abandon ship."

The aqua-evac pods—emergency evacuation craft—were their only chance for escape. Milo followed Audrey, Dr. Sweet, Rourke, and the other crew members into one of the three large vehicles on the sub's launch deck.

"Move it, people!" Helga shouted as she ushered the crew into the pods. "Sometime today would be nice! C'mon! Everybody grab a seat and buckle in!"

"Lieutenant," Rourke called as soon as everyone was accounted for, "get us out of here!"

Helga nodded and grabbed the release lever. She gave it a hard tug. It wouldn't budge.

"Lieutenant!" Rourke barked impatiently. Through the aqua-evac's small windows, they could see the giant Leviathan closing in on their crippled sub.

"I'm working on it!" Helga snapped back. She grunted and pulled on the lever. Finally, she stepped back and gave it an angry, desperate kick.

The release lever snapped back, and the exit bay doors opened wide. The three aqua-evac vehicles shot out into the deep, icy water. But their troubles were far from over.

Behind them, the Leviathan crushed their submarine into pieces. Then the mechanical monster turned and followed the aqua-evacs.

Commander Rourke turned to Milo. "Where to, Mr. Thatch?" he demanded.

Milo riffled through the pages of the Journal. "We're looking for a big crevice of some kind," he said with a hopeful shrug.

Rourke stared across the ocean floor and suddenly pointed. "There! Up ahead!" he called.

Milo stepped up and peered over his shoulder. Sure enough, there was a crack in the sea floor, just large enough for their ship to slip through.

Helga steered her vehicle toward the crevice. "All craft make your mark twenty degrees down angle," she radioed to the pilots of the other aqua-evacs and the subpods.

At the same time, Vinny and Mole and the other subpod pilots were doing their best to follow Helga's lead. But the angry Leviathan was making that very hard to do. One by one, it crushed the fleeing vehicles in its tremendous claws and exploded them with lethal electric rays.

"We're getting killed out here!" one pilot radioed. Frantically, he tried to follow Helga and Vinny's vehicles as they finally reached the crevice and entered a long, narrow underwater tunnel. The Leviathan could not follow the vehicles through the small crack. Instead, it fired an electric beam that hit the subpod bringing up the rear. The pod spun out of control and crashed into one of the other aqua-evacs. With a deafening *KA-BOOM,* both vehicles exploded in a single fiery ball.

Helga made it through the tunnel and into an air-filled underwater cave. Her ship and Mole and Vinny's sub-pod were the only ones that had come through safely.

Cautiously, the remaining crew climbed out of their vehicles and surveyed the surroundings. A searchlight from the ship shone on a giant carved dragon's head, which marked the beginning of the ancient highway to Atlantis. They had found it! But they had lost many men and women in the process.

Once they were all ashore, the crew took a moment to remember their fallen comrades. Dr. Sweet lit a candle and set it afloat on the water, nestled inside a helmet.

"Seven hours ago," Commander Rourke began, "we started this expedition with two hundred of the finest men and women I've ever known." He looked at the few dozen people standing around him. "We're all that's left.

"I won't sugarcoat it," he went on. "We have a crisis on our hands. But we've been up this creek before and we've always come through, paddle or no paddle. I see no reason to change that policy now. Looks like all our chances for survival rest with you, Mr. Thatch." His eyes moved to the Journal, tucked under Milo's arm. "You and that little book."

Milo swallowed hard. Mrs. Packard shook her head.

"We're all gonna die," she said with a sigh.

# CHAPTER 5

**M**ilo and the crew readied themselves to finish what they'd started. They unloaded the convoy of land vehicles that had been stowed inside the aqua-evac and prepared for the next leg of their journey to Atlantis.

"Okay, people," Commander Rourke shouted, "saddle up! Lieutenant, I want this convoy moving five minutes ago."

Helga nodded and whistled and the line of vehicles set off. Slowly, they rumbled through dark, winding caves. For miles and miles, they made their way through the damp, dreary darkness.

In the meantime, Milo was having a tough time proving himself to his crewmates. His attempt at driving one of the vehicles in the convoy was a colossal disaster. He led the expedition off course and directly to a vicious cave beast while he navigated with the Journal upside down. And Vinny played his favorite practical joke on Milo, tricking him into thinking he had sipped nitroglycerin from a canteen. Milo temporarily won Audrey's respect when he fixed the stalled digger with a whack of the wrench. But he wasn't sure he would ever be accepted as one of the crew.

Nonetheless, the convoy continued, and Milo took comfort in the fact that they were getting closer to Atlantis. Soon they found themselves gazing out over a great gorge. They parked their trucks at the edge of a bridge spanning the dark abyss and stared up at a large glowing rock formation that hung from the cave ceiling.

"This is it. It's gotta be!" Milo exclaimed. The gateway to the city of Atlantis—just as the Journal had described it!

"Why is it glowing?" Audrey asked.

"It is a natural phosphorescence," Mole said, then explained that chemicals in the rock made it give off light.

"That thing is gonna keep me up all night," Vinny complained. "I know it."

The crew set up camp where they were. They had traveled a long way and they needed food and rest.

While they pitched their tents and laid out bedrolls, Cookie got busy fixing the evening meal.

"Come and get it!" he finally cried as he rolled into camp with a cart full of grub. "For the appetizer . . . Caesar salad, escargot, and yer oriental spring rolls."

Audrey stepped up and sighed as she held her plate out to be filled with grayish grub.

"*I* wanted the escargot!" Mole complained over her shoulder.

Audrey shrugged and traded plates with him. "Knock yourself out," she said, rolling her eyes.

"There ya go, Milo," said Cookie, piling a ladleful of mush onto Milo's plate. "Put some meat on them bones!"

Milo tried to look grateful and find something positive to say. "Thanks, Cookie—that looks, uh . . . greasier than usual."

Cookie's face broke into a wide grin. "You like it?" he said, surprised. Then he picked up the whole pot of chow and dumped it onto Milo's plate. "Well, have some more! You're so skinny, if you turned sideways and stuck out your tongue, you'd look like a zipper."

While the rest of the crew howled with laughter, Milo slinked off to eat yet another meal alone. It seemed no matter how hard he tried to fit in with the others, they continued to treat him like one big, skinny joke.

From across the camp, Dr. Sweet watched Milo sit down with his tray and the Journal. "You know, we've been pretty tough on the kid," he told the others. "Whaddaya say we cut him some slack?"

Audrey looked up from their cozy campfire. "Yeah, you're right," she said with a nod. "Hey, Milo!" she called. "Why doncha come sit with us?"

Milo perked up at the invitation. "Really?" he called back. "You don't mind?"

"Nah," said Audrey, patting the rock between her and Mole. "Park it here."

Milo stood up and carried his book and tray over. "Gee," he said, taking a seat beside Mole, "this is great. I mean, you know, it's an honor to be included in your—"

*Pfffthhhtttt!*

Milo jumped up, red-faced, and turned around. Someone had put a hot water bottle on the rock just before he sat down.

"MOLE!" Doctor Sweet, Vinny, and Audrey cried out together.

"Ah, forgive me," Mole said between bouts of hysterical laughter. "I could not resist!"

Audrey glared and gave him a good jab with her elbow. Then she turned back to Milo. "Hey, Milo," she said, pointing toward *The Shepherd's Journal,* "don't you ever close that book?"

"Yeah," said Dr. Sweet, "you must have read it a dozen times by now."

Milo nodded as he sat down a second time. He opened his book and pointed to a long coded passage. "I know . . . but this doesn't make sense. See, in this passage here, the shepherd seems to be leading up to something. He calls it the Heart of Atlantis. It could be the power source the legends refer to, but then it just cuts off." He frowned and scratched his head. "It's almost like there's a missing page."

Vinny leaned over and patted Milo on the shoulder. "Kid, relax. We don't get paid overtime."

"I know, I know." Milo sighed. "Sometimes I get a little carried away. But, hey," he said as he smiled at the crew around him, "that's what it's all about, right? I mean discovery, teamwork, adventure?

Unless maybe you're just in it for the money?''

The crew looked at each other.

Audrey raised her hand. "Money," she said.

Mrs. Packard nodded. "Money."

"Money," Mole declared.

"Money," agreed the doctor.

Vinny thought for a moment, then had to agree. "I'm gonna say money."

Milo sighed again. "Well, I guess I set myself up for that one." Then he wearily rubbed his neck.

"Something wrong with your neck?" Sweet asked.

"Ah, yeah," Milo told him. "I must have hurt it when— YAHHH! GAHHH!"

Milo howled as the doctor grabbed him from behind, wrapped his thick arms around Milo's head, and twisted.

"Better?" the doctor asked.

Milo stood speechless for a moment. Then, slowly, he turned his head this way and that. "Yeah," he said, surprised. The pain was gone. "Hey, where'd you learn how to do that?"

"An Arapahoe medicine man." Sweet grinned.

"Get outta here."

"Born and raised with them," the doctor said,

nodding. "My father was an army medic. He settled down in the Kansas Territory after he met my mother."

Sweet pulled a worn photo out of his wallet and showed it to Milo. There, not quite smiling, was a tall African American man in a uniform with a pretty Native American woman by his side.

"No kidding," said Milo.

"Nope." Sweet shook his head. "I got a sheepskin from Howard U. and a bearskin from ol' Iron Cloud. Halfway through medical school, I was drafted. One day I'm studying gross anatomy in the classroom. The next I'm sewing up Rough Riders on San Juan Hill."

Just then Cookie rolled up with another steaming cart.

"Main course," he announced.

Vinny shook his head as the sour smell wafted toward him. "I couldn't eat another bite," he said, and patted his stomach.

Cookie shrugged and moved on to Mrs. Packard.

"Oh, no. I'll pass," she told him. "I had a big lunch."

"Oh, no." Dr. Sweet cringed. "No, no, no, no. Don't make me, don't ask me."

"Thanks anyway," said Audrey. "But, uh, I'm watching my weight."

Cookie nodded with understanding. "Don't you worry," he assured them as he rolled the cart away. "It'll keep and keep and keep."

"Thank God I lost my sense of taste years ago," Mrs. Packard mumbled.

By then, it was time for the hungry crew to get some shut-eye. Milo changed into his pajamas and stood staring at the pile of canvas at his feet.

"Aren't you gonna pitch up your tent?" Vinny asked as he walked by.

"Uh. . . I did," Milo said. "Guess I'm still a little rusty at this. I haven't been camping since the last time Grandpa took me."

Vinny shook his head. Then with a pull here and a tug there, he organized Milo's tent into a freestanding, functional structure.

As they were turning in for the night, Audrey asked Milo what it was like having Thaddeus Thatch for a grandfather.

Milo smiled wistfully and sighed. "Where do you start?" he replied. "He was like a father to me, really. My parents died when I was a little kid, and he took me in."

Then Milo chuckled to himself.

"What?" Audrey asked.

"I was just thinking. One time when I was eight, we were hiking along this stream, and I saw something shining in the water. It was a genuine arrowhead. Well, you'd think I'd found a lost civilization the way Grandpa carried on about it."

Milo laughed again fondly. "It wasn't until I was older that I realized the arrowhead was just some compressed shale mixed with zinc pyrite that had fractured into an isoceletic triangulate."

"Ha, ha," said Mole with a soft, sentimental chuckle. "That is so cute."

There was silence for a moment; then Milo spoke up. "Say, Audrey, no offense, but how does a teenager become the chief mechanic of a multimillion-dollar expedition?"

Audrey shrugged. "Well, I took this job when my dad retired. But the funny thing was, he always wanted sons, right? One to run his machine shop, and one to be middleweight boxing champion. But he got my sister and me instead."

"So what happened to your sister?" Milo asked.

Audrey grinned. "She's 24 and 0, with a shot at the title next month. Anyway, I'm saving up so my Poppy and I can open another shop."

"Well, as far as me goes," said Vinny, offering his own life story, "I just like to blow stuff up." The demolitions expert smoothed his shaggy mustache.

"Come on, Vinny." Dr. Sweet nudged his shoulder. "Tell the kid the truth."

"My family owned a flower shop," Vinny confessed. "We would sell roses, carnations, baby's breath—you name it. One day, I'm making about three dozen corsages for this prom—you know, the one they put on their wrists. And everybody, they come. 'Where is it? When is it? Does it match my dress?'" He shook his head in disgust. "It's a nightmare. Anyway, I guess there was this leak next door—of gas or what—*BOOM!* No more Chinese laundry. Blew me right through the front window. It was like a sign from God." Vinny held his palms up to the sky. "I found myself, that boom."

Just then, some dirt landed on Milo's nose. He turned and spotted Mole digging himself in for the night.

Milo nodded toward the commotion. "What's Mole's story?" he asked the others.

Dr. Sweet shook his head matter-of-factly. "Trust me on this one," he said. "You don't want to know."

Audrey opened her mouth to say something. But the doctor cut her off.

"Audrey, don't tell him," he warned her. "You shouldn't have told me, but you did. And now I'm telling you, Milo, you don't want to know."

# CHAPTER 6

"**W**ha—hmmm?"

Milo started from his sleep with a strong and very funny feeling that someone was watching him. Drowsily he looked around inside his tent. Nothing. No one.

He fumbled in the dark for a shovel, a flashlight, and a roll of toilet paper, and tiptoed out of his tent.

He waited until he was some distance from the tents before he switched his flashlight on. The bright beam illuminated the glimmering cave wall, then traveled up the ceiling to the rock chandelier suspended from the cave ceiling.

*Zwoop! Zwaap!* Milo watched in awe as a swarm of fireflies emerged from the rock formation—awakened by the flashlight beam. At first, they were a beautiful sight, as they twinkled and glowed and drifted toward Milo. Moments later, he was shocked as a few of them landed on his tent, instantly setting it on fire. Then more fireflies landed on other tents, with the same result. Within seconds the whole camp was ablaze.

*"Fiirre! Fiiirrrre!"* Milo yelled, trying to rouse the crew.

"Thatch," growled Rourke as he groggily stepped out of his tent. Then he spotted the leapfrogging flames—and his fleeing crew.

"Get some water on that fire!" Helga shouted as she too dashed out of her tent.

"No time!" Rourke called out. He pointed to some smaller caves across the narrow stone bridge. "Get us into those caves. Move it, move it, move it!"

As quickly as they could, the crew climbed into their vehicles and started across the bridge.

*Faster, faster,* Milo thought.

Then, just as Mole's digger had almost reached the other side, a group of fireflies landed on the fuel truck. It ignited in a fiery flash, and the force of the explosion broke the ancient bridge in two.

"No! No! No!" Mole cried out as his digger began to

slide backward. Frantically, he tried to switch gears. But it was no use. The digger was going down, and it was taking the rest of the convoy with it.

"No! No! *No!*"


It was dark. Pitch black. Slowly the silence that had followed the wreck was broken by moans and groans. They had ended up—vehicles and all—at the bottom of a cavern. And luckily it had been a relatively soft landing.

"All right," Commander Rourke's deep voice finally called out. "Who's not dead—sound off!"

One by one, the crew moaned in response.

"Oh, *mi cabeza*. My head," Audrey said with a groan.

"Dang lightnin' bugs done bit me on my sit-upon," Cookie complained. "Somebody's gonna have to suck out the poison. Now, don't nobody jump up at once."

"That's it," said Sweet. "I quit."

"Audrey, give me a damage report!" Rourke commanded.

Audrey's flashlight clicked on.

"Not as bad as it could have been," she declared as she cast her light across the wreckage. "We totaled rigs number two and seven, but the digger looks like it'll still run. Lucky for us, we landed in something soft."

Mole leaned over and put his ear to the ground. "Pumice ash . . . ," he said with a nod. "We are standing at the base of a dormant volcano."

Helga reached into her pack for a flare gun and fired it up and into the darkness. The crew watched the fiery ball shoot up . . . and up . . . and up.

"It just keeps going," Helga said.

Vinny looked up hopefully. "Maybe that's our ticket outta here!"

Then—*THUNK!*—the flare hit the roof and fizzled out.

"Maybe not," muttered Helga.

Mole ran his pudgy hands lovingly through the ash. "The magma has solidified in the bowels of the volcano," he expertly observed, "effectively blocking the exit."

Rourke punched his fist into his hand. "If we could blow the top off that thing, we'd have a straight shot to the surface," he declared. "Mr. Thatch, what do you think?"

He waited for Milo's answer.

"Mr. Thatch? Thatch?"

Audrey shined her flashlight all around the deep, dark chamber.

Milo was nowhere to be seen.

No one, not even Milo, knew that he was in another nearby cave. He was lying unconscious on a rock as three mysterious masked warriors stood over him.

*"Toog poh YOO-geh-bin KHAH-ben-deh-toat,"* one warrior said finally. ("He's dressed so strangely.")

*"Luht suhl-DOO-peh-toat duhp?"* another one asked. ("Where did he come from?")

*"Toog KOO-net suhl-DOOP KHOH-peh-toat,"* answered the third, who seemed to be their leader. ("He must be from the surface.")

"But how did he get here?"

"Should we kill him?"

*"Kwahm,"* the third warrior told them. ("No. He doesn't appear to be hostile.")

With the tip of a spear, the warrior leader carefully lifted Milo's glasses off his face.

Milo's eyes fluttered open and he beheld the blurry vision of three giant masks staring at him. He tried to push himself to his feet—then grabbed his shoulder in pain.

"Ahhh!" he gasped as his hand came away covered in blood. He fell back, afraid.

The third warrior slowly put a hand up and pulled

off the mask. Milo found himself face to face with a wide-eyed young woman. She had long blond—almost white—hair and a bright blue tattoo just under her left eye. Milo couldn't help noticing that she was the most beautiful girl he had ever seen.

For a moment, the two stared at each other without moving or saying a word. Then the warrior took hold of a bright blue crystal hanging around her neck. Gently, she placed it on Milo's wound. When she pulled her hand away, Milo's shoulder was healed!

The sounds of drills and engines broke the silence. The three warriors jumped to their feet in alarm. And without another word, they raced off, climbing effortlessly over the rocky terrain, fleeing from Milo's approaching companions.

"Whoa . . . whoa!" Milo called after the warriors. "Hey, wait! Just a minute! Who are you? Come back!"

Milo got to his feet and tried to follow them. But it was too late. They had already disappeared.

Dazed and confused, and now standing on a rock ledge overlooking a misty vista, Milo hardly noticed the cave wall crumbling behind him, plowed to rubble by Mole and the digger.

"Sweet mother of Jefferson Davis!" Cookie exclaimed as the convoy rolled through.

"It's beautiful!" cried Audrey.

"Milo," said Dr. Sweet, beaming. The doctor stepped up and gave him a hearty slap on the back. "I gotta hand it to ya. You really came through."

But Milo did not answer. He stood speechless and breathless as the mist cleared and he found himself gazing at the awe-inspiring ruins of a once-great city.

They had found the lost empire of Atlantis!

Milo's mouth fell open. He could hardly believe his eyes. Spread out before him was the goal he had sought for so many years.

Before anyone could say another word, the group of masked warriors with long spears confronted the explorers.

"Holy cats!" Commander Rourke shouted. "Who are these guys?"

"They gotta be Atlanteans," Milo answered.

"What?" cried Helga. "That's impossible."

Cookie raised his bushy eyebrows. "I seen this back in the Dakota," he warned them. "They can smell fear just by lookin' at ya. So keep quiet."

In their strange language, one of the warriors spoke up. *"Leb EH-seh-nekh dupp DOO-weh-ren-toap? Luht sull-DOO-peh-nekh dupp?"* ("Who are you strangers and where are you from?")

Mole gave Milo a little nudge. "I think it's talking to you," he said.

Milo stepped forward. He was the linguistics expert, after all. He knew this was why he'd been brought along. He took a deep breath and tried to reply in Atlantean.

He started by repeating the warrior's question: *"Leb EH-seh-nekh dupp DOO-weh-ren-toap? Luht sull-DOO-peh-nekh dupp?"*

Slowly the warrior raised her mask and showed her face to the explorers. It was the girl who had healed Milo's wound!

"Your manner of speech is strange to me," she said in Atlantean.

Milo struggled for the right reply. He had spent years studying the ancient language. But somehow the words kept sticking in his throat.

"I . . . travel . . . friend . . ," he stammered.

"You are friendly traveler," the girl corrected him.

Milo nodded. *"Ita, sum amice viator,"* he said, switching nervously to Latin.

To his surprise, the girl responded in Latin. *"Dices linguam Romae."* ("You speak the language of the Romans.")

Milo gulped and nodded. *"Parlez-vous français?"* If she could speak Latin, he wondered, could she speak French, too?

*"Oui, monsieur!"* she said excitedly.

"They speak my language!" exclaimed Mole.

And with that, the Atlantean warriors began shouting greetings in every language they knew. *"Ciao. Shalom. Salut. Grüße. Yasu. Neehowma. Leehobo . . ."*

"How do they know all these languages?" Audrey asked Milo.

"Their language must be based on a root dialect," Milo guessed.

"Well," said Commander Rourke, "maybe English is in there somewhere." He took a step toward the Atlanteans. "We are explorers from the surface world," he announced. "We come in peace!"

At that, the girl warrior smiled and made a welcoming gesture toward the city behind her. "Welcome to the city of Atlantis," she said in perfect English. "Come. You must speak with my father."

And with a mix of shock and glee, the crew boarded the vehicles and prepared to follow the warriors to their city.

Inside the lead truck with Rourke and Helga, Milo could hardly contain his excitement.

". . . and what's really amazing is that if you deconstructed Latin, overlaid it with a little Sumerian, threw in a dash of Thessalonian, you'd be getting close to their basic grammatical structure. Or at least in the same ballpark. Which is almost exactly like certain obscure offshoots of Choctaw!"

"Someone's having a good time," Helga said with a nod toward Milo in the backseat.

"Like a kid at Christmas," Rourke agreed.

Helga lowered her voice. "Commander," she said with some concern, "there were not supposed to be people down here. This changes everything."

Rourke clenched his jaw and stared grimly at the road.

"This changes nothing," he replied.

# CHAPTER 7

**S**oon Milo, Rourke, and Helga found themselves in the center of Atlantis, inside a once-lavish throne room. The walls, however, had crumbled to the ground and the floor was cracked. As a result, it was hard to tell just where the room started and the jungle stopped.

They followed the female warrior toward the large carved throne. On it sat a frail and ancient-looking king. His long white beard hung down to his waist. Like the girl, he wore a bright blue crystal around his neck, and he had blue tattoos across his nose and forehead and on the backs of his hands. His eyes stared unseeingly ahead of him, as if peering into the distance.

"Greetings, Your Highness," the girl called in Atlantean as she led them forward. "I have brought the visitors."

The king turned his head in the direction of Kida's voice. "You know the law, Kida," he told her in their native language. "No outsiders may see the city and live."

"Father," she said earnestly, "these people may be able to help us."

The king leaned forward and gravely shook his head. "We do not need their help," he said.

"But, Father—"

The king raised his hand. "That is enough!" he snapped. "We will discuss this later."

"Ahem." Commander Rourke stepped up and cleared his throat. "Your Majesty," he said with a bow, "on behalf of my crew, may I say it is an honor to be welcomed to your city?"

Anxiously, Milo tugged on Rourke's sleeve. "Excuse me, Commander?" he whispered. Only Milo had been able to understand the conversation thus far between the girl and the king. Rourke had no idea that they were not welcome.

But Rourke just shook him off.

"You presume too much to think you are welcome here," the king replied to Rourke in English.

"But, sir," Rourke protested, "we have come a long way looking for—"

"I know what you seek," the king broke in. "And you will not find it here. Your journey has been in vain."

Milo shifted uncomfortably as Rourke continued his argument. "But we are peaceful explorers," he went on, "men of science—"

"And yet you bring weapons," the king interrupted.

"Our weapons allow us to remove *obstacles* we may encounter," Rourke explained.

The king let out a long, weary sigh. "Some obstacles cannot be removed with a mere show of force," he said. "Return to your people. You must leave Atlantis at once."

Milo's shoulders fell in disappointment. He had hoped they might be able to stay and learn more about these people and their culture. But he had no desire at all to be where he wasn't wanted.

To his dismay, Rourke challenged the king.

"Your Majesty," Rourke begged, "be reasonable."

"Sir," Milo whispered.

"Not now, son."

"Trust me on this," Milo urged him. "We better do as he says."

But Rourke shrugged him off once more and addressed the king. "May I respectfully request that we stay one night, sir? My men are exhausted. That would give us time to rest, resupply, and be ready to travel by morning."

The king stroked his beard and thought for a moment. "Very well," he grumbled. "One night. That is all."

"Thank you, Your Majesty!" Rourke said as a satisfied smile spread across his face.

As the explorers left the room, the king's strength gave out and he lay down on his bed. The tense exchange with Rourke had exhausted him. The old man had lived for more than twenty thousand years, and now it was clear that his days were coming to an end.

His daughter sat on the edge of his bed and took his hand.

"Your heart has softened, Kida," he told her. "A thousand years ago you would have slain them on sight."

A sadness fell over her face. "A thousand years ago the streets were lit and our people did not have to scavenge for food at the edge of a crumbling city."

"The people are content," the king told her.

"They do not know any better!" she argued. "We were once a great people. Now we live in ruins. The kings of our past would weep if they could see how far we have fallen."

"Kida—"

"If these outsiders can unlock the secrets of our past," Kida went on, "perhaps we can save our future."

The king shook his head. "What they have to teach us, we have already learned."

"Our way of life is dying!" Kida exclaimed.

The king patted the hand of his passionate daughter. "Our way of life is preserved," he said simply. "Kida, when you take the throne, you will understand."

Meanwhile, Rourke, Helga, and Milo had rejoined the rest of their crew on the steps of the throne room.

"So, how'd it go?" Dr. Sweet asked.

"The king and his daughter don't exactly see eye to eye," Milo answered. "She seems to like us okay, but the king . . . I don't know, I think he's hiding something."

Rourke folded his arms across his chest. "Well, if he's hiding something, I want to know what it is."

"Someone needs to talk to that girl," Helga declared.

Eagerly, Mole raised his hand. But the commander

already had someone else in mind for the job.

He reached out and gave Milo's hand a hearty shake. "Good man, Thatch," he told the stunned explorer. "Thanks for volunteering."

# CHAPTER 8

**W**hile Milo waited for Kida to come out of the king's chambers, he went over what he would say for the hundredth time.

He took a deep, nervous breath. "Okay, Milo," he told himself, "don't take no for an answer. 'Look, I have some questions for you, and I'm not leaving this city until they're answered.' Yeah, yeah, that's it, that's good, that's good."

He felt a hand clamp down over his mouth.

"I have some questions for you and you are not leaving the city until they are answered," a voice commanded. It was Kida.

Milo spun around, stunned and not sure what to say. "Yeah, w-well," he stammered, "I . . . okay."

"Shhh!" Kida ordered as she grabbed him by the arm. "Come with me."

The princess led Milo away from the palace and through the crumbling streets of Atlantis.

At last they came to a pile of glowing rocks on the outskirts of the city. As Milo watched, Kida pushed aside the largest one—to reveal a cave full of more broken statues, faded carvings, and what looked to Milo like strange tools and machines. What was this place?

She turned to him. "There is so much to ask about your world. You are a scholar, are you not?" She looked him over from head to toe. "Judging from your diminished physique and large forehead, you are suited for nothing else. What is your country of origin? When did the floodwaters recede? How did you—"

"Wait a minute," Milo cut in. "I've got a few questions for you, too," he said, talking quickly and excitedly. "Let's do this, okay? You ask one. Then I'll ask one. Then you, then me, and then . . ." He paused for breath. "Well . . . you get it."

"Very well." Kida nodded. "What is your first question?"

Milo thought for a second. "Well, okay. How did you get here?"

Kida looked at him, puzzled.

"Well, I mean, not you personally, but your culture. I mean, how did all of this end up down here?"

Kida shrugged. "It is said that the gods became jealous of Atlantis. They sent a great cataclysm and banished us here. All I can remember is the sky going dark and people shouting and running. Then a bright light, like a star, floating above the city. My father said it called my mother to it." Her large blue eyes filled with tears. "I never saw her again."

"I'm sorry," Milo said. "If it's any consolation, I know how you feel. I lost my. . .Wait a minute—back up. You remember? I mean you were there? That's impossible. I mean, that would make you more than . . . eight *thousand* years old!"

Kida nodded.

Milo's face cleared. "Oh, well, uh, hey, looking good," he said good-naturedly. "Uh, do you have another question for me?"

"How is it you found your way to this place?"

Milo grinned. "I'll tell you, it wasn't easy." Then he

reached into his pack and pulled out the Journal. "If it weren't for this book," he said, giving it a pat, "we never would have made it."

He handed the book to Kida, then went on with his questioning.

"Okay," he said, "second question. Legend has it that you people were far more advanced in the areas of science and technology—"

"You mean," Kida broke in as she leafed through the Journal, "you can understand this?"

Milo nodded and shrugged. "Yes, I'm a linguist— that's what I do, that's my job. Now, getting back to my question—"

"This," Kida repeated, pointing to a printed page. "Right here, you can read this?"

"Yes! Yes!" Milo shouted impatiently. "I can read Atlantean just like you."

Kida stared back at him blankly.

Then suddenly Milo realized what Kida was trying to tell him. "You can't read it, can you?" he said, amazed.

"No one can," she told him. "Such knowledge has been lost to us since the time of the *MEH-behl-moak*."

"Oh, the Great Flood," said Milo, translating.

Kida nodded. Then she pointed to the page, eager to

learn its secret. "Show me," she said.

Milo moved to stand beside her. He ran his finger along a line of text. *"LEH-weg-tem SHEE-buhn puhk BEN-tem DEE-gen-mil SAH-tib. Yoos KEH-ruhn-tem SHAHD-luhg KOAM-tib-loh-nen."*

"'Follow the narrow passage for another league,'" Kida translated. "'There you will find the fifth marker.'"

"Yeah," Milo told her, "that's it."

Kida grabbed Milo's arm. "Here," she said, "let me show you something!"

She dragged him to a corner of the cave and lifted up a dusty tarp. Underneath was a big, stone . . . Milo wasn't sure what. It appeared to be a cross between a fish and a motorcycle.

"It looks like some sort of vehicle," he guessed.

Kida nodded but looked puzzled. "Yes, but no matter what I try, it will not respond. Perhaps if—"

Milo held up his hand. "Way ahead of you," he said. He pointed to the writing carved into the side of the vehicle. "Let's see what we got here. Okay. 'Place crystal into slot . . .'"

"Yes, yes." Kida nodded again. "I have done that."

"'Gently place your hand on the inscription pad.'"

"Yes," said Kida.

"Okay, did you turn the crystal one quarter turn back?"

"Yes, yes."

"While your hand was on the inscription pad?"

"Ye—No."

"Well, there's your problem right there," Milo told her. "That's an easy thing to miss. You know, you deserve credit for even getting this far."

Kida flashed him a look of annoyance. With a flip of her platinum hair, she did everything the inscription said: she placed her blue crystal in the slot, laid her other hand on the pad, and turned the crystal one quarter turn back.

*ZAP!*

Instantly, a burst of blue energy lit the stone vehicle from within. And with a tiny shudder it hovered just above the ground.

"*YAHD-lu-goh-nikh!*" Kida exclaimed. ("Good heavens!")

"Yeah! You got that right!" agreed Milo. "With this thing, I can see the whole city in no time at all! I wonder how fast it goes." He reached out and placed his hand on the hovering fish.

*ZOOM!*

The next thing Milo knew, the speeder was zipping

around the cave and bouncing off the walls. Both he and Kida dove to the ground to get out of the way—and not a moment too soon! The vehicle narrowly missed their heads, then hit the ground and lodged in the sand.

"So," said Milo jokingly, "who's hungry?"

After that near miss, Milo decided there was a lot to be said for going on foot. So Kida took him on a walking tour of her city.

First they climbed to the top of a giant stone statue—one of several lying throughout Atlantis. "We were never properly introduced," Milo said to the princess as they climbed. He grinned and stretched out his hand. "My name is Milo."

Kida smiled and shook his hand. "My name is Kidagakash," she said.

"Kidagashma . . ." Milo stumbled over the syllables. "You got a nickname?"

She laughed and nodded. "Kida."

"Okay, Kida. I can remember that." Milo smiled.

From the top of the statue they could see the entire city. The view took Milo's breath away. As Kida eyed him closely, he reached up and brushed a tear from his face.

"What is wrong?" Kida asked.

"Oh, nothing . . . nothing," he replied. "I just got something in my eye." But he was beginning to feel that he could talk to Kida. "Ya know, my grandpa used to tell me stories of this place as far back as I can remember. I just wish he could be standing here with me."

Wherever Grandpa Thaddeus was, Milo knew he was smiling. Milo recalled all the hours spent with his grandfather, listening to his stories of Atlantis and picturing the magical place in his mind. Now here he was, gazing at a breathtaking view of the lost empire.

And their tour had barely begun. Milo sampled Atlantean food. (Blue—but rather tasty!) He played with Atlantean pets. (Who knew baby whales with feet could be so cute?) And he met lots of Atlantean people. The Great Flood had destroyed their world, but it had not destroyed their spirit.

Together, Kida and Milo strolled around a tranquil pool, trying to catch fireflies.

"You know, Kida," said Milo, "the most we ever hoped to find here was some crumbling buildings, maybe some broken pottery. Instead, we find a living, thriving society."

Kida shook her head sadly. "We are not thriving," she

replied. "True, our people live, but our culture is dying. We are like a stone the ocean beats against. With each passing year, a little more of us is worn away."

"I wish there was something I could do."

Kida looked him in the eye. "I have brought you to this place to ask you for your help. There is a mural here with writing all around the pictures."

Milo grinned. "Well, you came to the right guy. How 'bout we start with this column right here?" He pointed to an engraved pillar beside them, then turned to get Kida's attention. "Uh, Kida . . . what are you doing?" His mouth fell open as he watched Kida step out of her skirt.

"You do swim, do you not?" she said.

"Oh . . ." Milo took a deep breath. "I swim pretty good."

"Good," said Kida, laying her skirt on the grass. "It is a fair distance to where we are going."

"Hey, you're talking to the belly flop champ at Camp Runamuck."

Moments later, Kida was leading Milo on an entirely different tour—this one through the underwater ruins of another part of Atlantis. To Milo, it was just as lovely—and even more mysterious.

After about a minute, though, he started to get nervous. Kida might have been used to swimming for miles underwater. But he was not!

Luckily, just when he thought his lungs would explode, Kida led him to a pocket of air. He burst to the surface, gasping for breath.

"Are you all right?" Kida asked.

"Well, I didn't drown."

"Good," said Kida. "Follow me."

Milo watched her dive back under, and reluctantly he followed. But when he saw where she was taking him, he almost forgot about breathing altogether.

It looked to him like some kind of temple. The walls were covered with huge, elaborate murals. And if he was translating them right, they told the entire history of Atlantis.

Excitedly, Milo motioned to Kida to swim up for air once again.

"This is amazing!" he exclaimed as they broke the surface in the air pocket. "A complete history of Atlantis! It's just like Plato described it. Well, he was off on a few details."

Kida nodded eagerly. "The light I saw. The star, in the middle of the city. What does the writing say about that?"

"I don't know yet," Milo told her. "But we're gonna find out! Come on."

He took her by the hand and they dove once again. This time, Milo used Kida's glowing crystal necklace to help light up the wall.

He stopped in front of a drawing that showed a large blue crystal falling from the sky. Then he moved on to a picture showing citizens of Atlantis wearing small pieces of the Crystal around their necks.

"The Heart of Atlantis!" he declared as they went up for air a third time.

"What?" asked Kida.

"It's the Heart of Atlantis! That's what the shepherd was talking about. It wasn't a star, it was—it was some kind of crystal, like these!" He pointed to the crystal around her neck.

"Don't you get it?" he said. "The power source I've been looking for, the bright light you remember, they're the same thing!"

He stared at her, beaming, and waited for her to reply.

"That cannot be," she said finally.

"It's what's keeping all of these smaller crystals . . . you . . . all of Atlantis alive!"

"Then where is it now?" she asked.

"I don't know! I don't know." Milo frowned and shook his head. "You'd think something this important would have been in the Journal. Unless . . . the missing page!"

Milo grabbed Kida's hand once more. He was going to figure this mystery out!

# CHAPTER 9

Underwater, Milo and Kida made their way back to the pool where they'd jumped in.

Milo was the first to reach the surface—and the first to find Commander Rourke and the rest of the crew waiting for them.

"You have a nice swim?" Rourke called.

"Hey, guys!" Surprised, Milo waved. "What's going on?" Then he noticed that each of his crewmates was carrying a weapon.

"What's—what's with all the guns?" he asked.

There was no answer.

"Guys?"

Then, suddenly, everything clicked in Milo's brain. The missing Journal page. The Heart of Atlantis. It all made sense.

"I'm such an idiot," said Milo, shaking his head. He looked up at Rourke with both anger and disappointment. "This is just another treasure hunt for you. And you're after the Crystal!"

The commander grinned and pulled a sheet of paper out of his boot. Even from the water, Milo could see that it was the missing page from *The Shepherd's Journal.*

"Oh, you mean this?" Rourke waved it teasingly.

Milo glared. "The Heart of Atlantis."

"Yeah, about that," Rourke explained. "I would have told you sooner, but it was strictly on a need-to-know basis." He grinned. "And, well, now you know. I had to be sure you were one of us."

Then he held out his hand to Milo. "Welcome to the club, son!"

But Milo turned away. "I'm no mercenary," he said.

Just then, Kida swam up beside him—and instantly one of Rourke's troopers grabbed her by the hair. Milo stood waist-deep in the water, too stunned to offer help. But Kida didn't need it.

She grabbed the soldier by his head and flipped him into the pool. A second soldier rushed at her, but in the blink of an eye, Kida was holding his gun and pistol and had him pinned to the ground.

Skillfully, she drew a knife from her belt and prepared to finish the soldier off. But just as she lowered her arm, a shot rang out and the blade went sailing into the water.

Rourke blew on the barrel of his smoking gun and ordered two more troopers forward.

"Mercenary?" Rourke looked at Milo. "I prefer the term 'adventure capitalist.' Besides, you're the one who got us here. You led us right to the treasure chest."

"You don't know what you're tampering with, Rourke," Milo warned as he watched Rourke's soldiers drag Kida to the edge of the pool.

"What's to know?" Rourke shrugged. "It's big, it's shiny, it's going to make us all rich!"

Milo knew there was no hope of reasoning with such greed. But he still had to try.

"You think it's some kind of diamond," he told Rourke. "I thought it was some kind of battery. But we're both wrong. It's their life force. That Crystal is the only thing keeping these people alive. You take that away and they'll die."

Rourke scratched his head with his pistol and turned to his second-in-command. "Well, that changes things. Helga, whaddaya think?"

Helga considered the question. "Knowing that," she said with a smile, "I'd double the price."

"I was thinking triple." Rourke laughed.

"Rourke, don't do this," Milo pleaded.

"I gotta admit I'm disappointed," Rourke replied. "You're an idealist. Just like your grandfather. Do yourself a favor, Milo. Don't be like him. For once, do the smart thing."

He paused to give Milo a chance to reply. But Milo just stared right through Rourke.

"I really hate it when negotiations go sour." Rourke sighed.

Then he snapped his fingers and two troopers grabbed Kida and pushed her down.

"Let's try this again."

Minutes later, Rourke and the crew burst into the king's chamber, carrying guns, dynamite, and Kida.

Immediately, two of the king's armed guards rushed toward them. But they halted when Helga held her gun to Kida's head.

"Tell them to drop their weapons. Now!" she told the king.

"Do as she says," the king commanded in Atlantean.

Helga nodded toward the others. "Spread out!" she shouted. "Search everywhere for that Crystal!"

Obediently, the soldiers and the crew began turning the throne room upside down.

When their search yielded nothing, Rourke grabbed Milo by the throat.

"You're not applying yourself, son," he hissed. "There's got to be something else."

"Well, there isn't," Milo said with a gasp. He pointed to the open Journal. "It just says, 'The Heart of Atlantis lies in the eyes of her king.'"

"Well, then," growled Rourke as he fixed his eyes on the frail king, "maybe ol' King Cole here can help us fill in the blanks."

He yanked the Journal from Milo's hands and made his way to the throne.

"How about it, Chief?" he called. "Where's the Crystal chamber?"

The king sighed heavily. "You will destroy yourselves," he said gravely.

"Maybe I'm not being clear." Rourke's cruel eyes

narrowed and he gave the king a punch that sent him sprawling on the ground.

"I will kill you for that!" Kida shouted as she struggled to break away. But Helga's hold on her was too strong.

"Rourke," said Dr. Sweet, taking a step forward, "this was not part of the plan."

"Plan's changed, Doc," Rourke said coldly. "I'd suggest you put a bandage on that bleeding heart of yours. It doesn't suit a mercenary."

With that, he shot a warning glare at the rest of the crew. Then he stepped over the fallen king and sat down on his throne.

"Well, as usual, diplomacy has failed us," Rourke declared as he aimed his gun at the king's head. "Now, I'm going to count to ten and you're going to tell me where the Crystal is. One."

Rourke cocked his revolver. "Two. Nine. Te—"

Rourke stopped and a smirk spread across his face. He had spotted something—a bright blue beam of light falling from the ceiling. It shone directly on a calm reflecting pool in the middle of the throne room.

Milo followed Rourke's gaze and looked carefully at the stones arranged within the pool. Where had he seen that design before? Of course! The engraving on the cover of *The Shepherd's Journal*!

Rourke had noticed the pattern too. He held up the book. The two symbols matched perfectly!

"'The Heart of Atlantis lies in the eyes of her king,'" Rourke repeated to himself. "This is it! We're in."

Milo took a step forward. "Rourke," he pleaded again, "for the last time, you gotta listen to reason. You don't have the slightest idea of what this power is capable of."

"True," Helga called out as she dragged Kida toward the water. "But I could think of a few countries who'd pay anything to find out."

Rourke waded into the shallow water, followed by Milo and Helga with Kida, still struggling to get away.

The water they were standing in began to vibrate. Rourke continued to the center of the pool and stood squarely on the stone symbol. To his surprise, it began to sink!

"Hurry! Get on!" Rourke shouted to Milo and Helga. He pulled Milo onto the "aquavator" as Helga stepped on with Kida.

The rest of the crew looked on as the four of them slowly descended into the unknown.

"Jackpot!" Rourke exclaimed. They had descended into a great chamber below the throne room. Before them was another shallow reflecting pool. And high above them, surrounded by huge stones, floated the giant blue Crystal. This was it—the Heart of Atlantis!

Kida pointed to the protector stones, each one carved to look like a different face. "The kings of our past!" she cried. Then she fell to her knees in prayer. "Spirits of Atlantis," she uttered in Atlantean, "forgive me for defiling your chambers and bringing intruders into the land."

Commander Rourke rolled his eyes. "Thatch," he barked, "tell her to wrap it up. We got a schedule to meet."

Milo knelt down next to the princess. "Uh, Kida," he said softly, "I'm sorry." He felt so responsible—so guilty. At that moment, he wished he'd never heard of the city of Atlantis.

Meanwhile, Rourke gazed smugly at his reflection in the pool. And with a greedy laugh, he kicked a pebble into the water.

Without warning, the Crystal above them flashed from blue to a fiery red—and crimson beams of light shot out like search beams. It was as if the Crystal had been awakened by Rourke's action.

"C'mon," Helga said nervously, "let's get this over with. I don't like this place."

Rourke nodded and aimed his gun at Milo. "All right, Thatch. What's next?"

Milo almost had to laugh at Rourke's arrogance. "Okay. There's a giant Crystal hovering one hundred and fifty feet above our heads over a bottomless pit of water. Doesn't anything surprise you?"

"The only thing that surprises me," Rourke replied, "is that you're still talking and that thing's not on the truck yet. Now, move it!"

Milo held up his hands. "I don't know how to move it," he said. "I don't even know what's holding it up there!"

Just then, the Crystal's red beam swept across the water and stopped when it reached Kida. Instantly, the beam turned blue. Kida seemed to fall into a sort of trance while the crystal around her neck began to float as if being pulled toward the larger Crystal.

"Talk to me, Thatch!" Rourke shouted. "What's happening?"

Milo watched as Kida began to walk stiffly to the edge of the pool. He glanced down at the open Journal, searching for an explanation.

"All it says here is the Crystal is alive somehow. I don't know how to explain it." He struggled to find the words for something he didn't even understand himself. "It's their deity. Their god. Their power source."

"Speak English, Professor," Rourke demanded snidely.

Milo raised his voice in utter frustration. "They're a part of it, and it's a part of them. I'm doing the best I can here!"

At that moment, Kida turned to face Milo. Her expression was as blank and empty as the faces of the King Stones hovering above them.

*"SOH-lesh MAH-toh-noat MY-loh THATCH-toap. Kwahm TEH-red-seh-nen,"* she said in Atlantean. ("All will be well, Milo Thatch. Be not afraid.") Milo saw the words coming from Kida's mouth, but he felt as if they were being spoken by some great voice far beyond her.

"What did she say?" Rourke asked angrily.

"I don't know," Milo lied. "I didn't catch it."

Then he watched Kida turn back and walk out onto the pool of water.

When she was directly under the Crystal, a blinding shaft of light beamed down on her. As Milo and the others looked on, Kida was lifted off the ground. She rose up and up and up, and unbelievably, she entered the Crystal itself!

"Kida," Milo murmured. He tried to step forward. But Commander Rourke held him back.

"Hold your horses, Loverboy," he said.

As they watched wide-eyed, the Crystal opened up—and Kida reappeared. She floated gently to the ground. She walked through the pool toward Milo, Rourke, and Helga. All at once, the protective King Stones that had surrounded the Crystal fell out of the air and splashed into the pool. As Kida neared the edge of the pool, Rourke reached out to grab her.

"No, don't!" Milo cried. "Don't touch her!" He could see that the crystal around her neck was glowing even more brightly than before. In fact, Kida's whole body seemed to be lit from within by the Crystal's blue light.

Something had changed in those few minutes. Milo could not explain why, but he now felt certain of one thing: Kida *was* the Crystal.

# CHAPTER 10

**R**ourke quickly realized the same thing as Milo. As far as he was concerned, Kida's transformation was not an obstacle. If the Crystal now resided in Kida, he would simply take Kida with him to the surface.

Carefully, the crystallized princess was brought up from the lower chamber and placed inside a special transport pod.

Milo watched sadly as Audrey sealed the pod and loaded it onto a truck. Then the explorers prepared to leave Atlantis and begin their journey home. A crowd of Atlanteans had gathered around. They stood nearby, stunned by what was happening but powerless against Rourke and his heavily armed troopers.

"Keep those people back!" Commander Rourke

ordered with a nasty sneer in Milo's direction.

"You heard him, step back," a trooper warned the Atlanteans and Milo.

"So, I guess this is how it ends, huh, Rourke?" Milo called. "Fine, you win. You're wiping out an entire civilization. But hey . . ." He shrugged. "You'll be rich."

Then he waved good-bye to the rest of the crew. Milo had expected so much more from them. "Congratulations, Audrey. Guess you and your dad will be able to open up that second garage after all. And Vinny, you—you can start a whole chain of flower shops. I'm sure your family's gonna be very proud. But that's what it's all about, right?" He shot them a disappointed glare. "Money."

"Get off your soapbox, Thatch," Rourke scoffed. "You've read Darwin. It's called natural selection. We're just helping it along."

Helga stepped out from the front of the convoy. "Commander!" she called. "We're ready!"

Rourke dealt Milo one final blow, a cruel sucker punch to the stomach. As Milo doubled over in pain, his glasses flew from his face. Rourke caught them in midair. He stood over Milo with a wicked grin on his face. "Look at it this way, son," he said. "You were the man who discovered Atlantis, and now you're part of the exhibit."

He tossed Milo his glasses, then waved his arm in a circle above his head. "Let's move, people!" he shouted.

He and Helga waited for the crew to take their places. But they seemed hesitant to follow Rourke.

"That was an order, not a suggestion," Helga prodded. "Let's go!"

But when the crew finally did move . . . it was to Milo's side!

Commander Rourke and Helga stared at them in disbelief.

"Oh, you can't be serious," Rourke said with a grimace.

Andrey crossed her arms in front of her. "This is wrong," she said simply, "and you know it."

Rourke's face began to twitch and turn red. "We're *this* close to our biggest payday ever and you pick now of all times to grow a conscience?" he roared.

Vinny nodded and crossed his arms as well. "We've done a lot of things we're not proud of," he said. "Robbing graves, plundering tombs, double parking.

But nobody got hurt." He thought for a moment. "Well, maybe somebody got hurt, but nobody we knew."

Rourke glared at the mutineers. Finally, he shrugged.

"Well, if that's the way you want it, fine," he spat. "More for me." And with that, he climbed into his truck and revved the engine.

Helga and the troopers followed his lead. They started up the line of trucks and headed out of the city, over a rope bridge, and toward the volcano shaft they had discovered on their way into Atlantis.

As he watched them leave, Milo's heart sank, and a harsh reality hit him with full force. He looked around at the crowd of Atlanteans. As Kida and the convoy went farther and farther away from the city, all the Atlanteans' individual crystals began to dim noticeably. How long would they survive without the life energy of the Crystal?

"We can't let him do this!" Milo cried.

But Vinny grabbed him by the waist and held him back. "Wait a minute," he said.

One second later—*BOOM!*—a massive explosion rang out and the bridge between Atlantis and the volcano crumbled. Vinny had been responsible for this part of Rourke's getaway plan.

"Okay, now you can go," Vinny said.

Milo's mouth fell open. But he didn't have time to worry about the ruined bridge. Another voice was calling to him from inside the palace.

"Milo! You'd better get up here!"

It was Dr. Sweet.

Milo looked down at the frail body of the king of Atlantis.

"How's he doing?" he asked the doctor.

Dr. Sweet shook his head. "Not good, I'm afraid. Internal bleeding. There's nothing more I can do."

Milo buried his head in his hands. "What a nightmare," he moaned. "And I brought it here."

"Ah, don't go beatin' yourself up," the doctor told him. "Rourke's been after that Crystal since Iceland."

"The Crystal." Milo's head suddenly perked up. "Sweet, that's it! These—these crystals—they have some sort of healing energy. I've—I've seen it work!"

At that moment, the king's eyes fluttered open and he reached for Milo's wrist.

"Where is my daughter?" he whispered between labored breaths.

Milo sighed and looked away. "Well, she, uh . . ."

But the king already knew the answer. "She has been chosen. Like her mother before her," he said slowly.

"What?" asked Milo.

The king gulped for air. "In times of danger, the Crystal will choose a host—one of royal blood—to protect itself and its people. It will accept no other."

Milo's eyes suddenly grew wide. "Wait a minute," he said. "*Choose?* So this thing is alive?"

Kida's father nodded weakly. "In a way. The Crystal thrives on the collective emotions of all who came before us. In return, it provides power, longevity, protection. As it grew, it developed a consciousness of its own."

The king sadly closed his eyes, and Milo leaned in closer to catch his words.

"In my arrogance, I sought to use it as a weapon of war, but its power proved too great to control. It overwhelmed us and led to our destruction."

"That's why you hid it beneath the city?" Milo asked him. "To prevent history from repeating itself?"

The king nodded. "And to prevent Kida from suffering the same fate as my beloved wife. The love of my daughter is all I have left. And my burden would have become hers when the time was right. But now . . ."

The king's eyes opened once more as he removed the crystal from his neck and pressed it into Milo's palm. ". . . it falls to you."

"Me?"

"Return the Crystal. Save the city. Save my daughter."

Milo opened his mouth to speak. There was so much he needed to ask the king. So much he still needed to know. But it was too late.

As Milo looked on, the king let out one final breath, and his weary eyes closed for the last time.

Sadly, Milo got up from the king's bed and clenched the small crystal in his fist.

Dr. Sweet gently arranged the king's body into a peaceful position. Then, as he stood up and closed his doctor's bag, he looked at Milo. "So, what's it going to be?"

"Excuse me?" Milo replied.

The doctor kept his eyes locked on Milo's. "I followed you in and I'll follow you out. It's your decision."

"Oh, my decision?" Milo rolled his eyes. "I—I think we've seen how effective my decisions have been! Let's recap: I lead a band of plundering vandals to the greatest archaeological find in recorded history, thus enabling the kidnap and/or murder of the royal family, not to mention personally delivering the most powerful force known to man into the hands of a mercenary nutcase who's probably gonna sell it to the Kaiser!" Milo took a deep breath. "Have I left anything out?"

"Well, you did set the camp on fire and drop us down that big hole," Sweet told him.

"Thank you. Thank you very much!"

Milo sat down and hung his head. *This is hopeless*, he thought. *No, this is utterly, eternally, insufferably hopeless. And it is all my fault.*

Dr. Sweet waited a moment, then knelt down by Milo's side. "Of course," he said, "it's been my experience, when you hit bottom, the only place left to go is up."

"Who told you that?" Milo asked bitterly.

"Fella by the name of Thaddeus Thatch."

At the mention of his grandfather's name, Milo raised his head.

Thaddeus Thatch had wanted Milo to finish the work he had begun. He had left Milo *The Shepherd's Journal* so that he could do just that. But he had also left Milo something else—his spirit. Thaddeus Thatch had never given up. And Milo wasn't going to either.

He took a deep breath. Then he held up the king's crystal, looking deep into its bright blue heart. He knew what he had to do.

# CHAPTER 11

**M**ilo stormed out of the palace, ready to take on anyone and anything. The crew and the crowd of Atlanteans were still gathered nearby, uncertain what to do next.

"Where ya goin'?" Audrey asked.

"I'm going after Rourke."

"Milo, that's crazy!" she argued.

But Milo just squared his shoulders and marched forward. "I didn't say it was the smart thing. But it's the right thing."

Audrey watched him walk by, then exchanged worried looks with Vinny.

"C'mon," she said with a nod in Milo's direction. "We better make sure he doesn't hurt himself."

Then they watched as Milo climbed onto a nearby

stone fish, similar to the one Kida had shown him in her secret cave.

"Milo, what do you think you're doing?" Audrey called.

"Just follow my lead!" Milo shouted.

He took the king's crystal pendant and stuck it in the keyhole. Then he placed his hand on the control pad and gave the crystal a quarter turn back.

In an instant, the vehicle was hovering in midair.

"Well, I'm impressed," Mrs. Packard said with an approving nod.

"It's simple." Milo told her. "All you gotta do is—"

"Yeah, yeah," Audrey cut in, jumping onto Milo's vehicle and shoving him out of the way. "We get it." Then she went to put her hand on the control pad.

"No, no, wait!" Milo shouted.

But it was too late. The fish went zooming backward and slammed into a wall.

"Gently," said Milo softly. "Just gently."

"Hey, Milo!" said Vinny, nodding at the fish-shaped flier. "You got something sporty? Ya know, like a tuna?"

Meanwhile, the Atlantean bystanders gasped in awe.

"How is this done?" one of them asked.

Milo hopped down from the vehicle and held up the

king's crystal. "All you gotta do is use the crystals," he explained. "Kida showed me."

Each of the Atlanteans hurried to claim a vehicle.

"Quarter turn back," Milo instructed as the Atlanteans placed their crystals in the key slots. "Keep your hand on the pad."

And within seconds, everyone was in the air. It was an important moment for Atlantis. This ancient fleet of vehicles—including Ketaks, Martags, and Aktiraks—had not been used for thousands of years.

"We're gonna make history or be history!" Milo cried as the *new* Atlantean armada zoomed across the sky. "Now, let's do it!"

Outside the city, at the base of the undersea volcano's shaft, Rourke was preparing to make his final getaway.

"I love it when I win," he said with a smirk as a cannon boomed and blasted a hole in the top of the sealed shaft.

Then he signaled a trooper in the tanker to open the huge wooden barrel on the back of the truck. Within seconds, an enormous hot-air balloon—the gyro-evac—was inflating and Rourke was attaching the transport pod, with Kida inside, to the bottom of it. This was the vehicle that would carry Rourke, Helga, and their treasure to the surface.

Meanwhile, Milo was formulating an attack strategy as the Atlantean armada neared Rourke's position.

"Here's the plan," he shouted as the fleet of vehicles sped through the air. "We're gonna come in low and fast and take 'em by surprise."

"I've got news for you, Milo," Audrey told him. "Rourke is never surprised, and he's got a lot of guns."

"Well, do you have any suggestions?" he asked.

"Yeah," said Vinny. "Don't get shot."

Just then, Rourke and his convoy came into view.

"There they are!" Milo yelled, pointing toward the dark volcano shaft. Rourke and Helga had already boarded the gyro-evac and had begun their ascent.

A shower of bullets came whizzing toward the armada. The Atlanteans fought back as best they could. But their primitive spears were no match for Rourke's guns—or for the nimble biplanes he was launching to fend off the attack.

It was Vinny who accidentally discovered the armada's secret weapon. He hit a small button on his control panel and—*ZAP!*—a lightning ray shot out from the front of the Martag and blasted away one of the troopers' trucks.

Vinny grinned and gave his Martag a friendly pat. "Okay!" he exclaimed with fire in his eyes. "Now things are getting good."

Soon all the Atlantean vehicles were firing lightning rays at the enemy, and Milo and his friends had a regular dogfight on their hands. But at the same time, Rourke's gyro-evac was rising, carrying Kida's pod with it. He was getting away!

"Vinny, heads up!" Milo yelled. "We can't let 'em reach the top of that shaft!"

As Atlantean vehicles and fighter planes flew around him, Milo watched Kida's pod floating farther and farther out of reach. He had to do something to save her and Atlantis—and he had to do it quickly!

"Vinny, new plan," Milo urgently called out. "You and me—we're gonna be decoys. Sweet, Audrey . . ."

"We're on it!" the doctor yelled.

Together, Audrey and Dr. Sweet steered their Martag so that it hovered beside the pod. Then Audrey took the doctor's saw and tried to cut through the thick chains that held the pod.

"I thought you said this thing could cut through a

femur in twenty-eight seconds!" Audrey huffed at the doctor.

"Less talk, more saw!" Dr. Sweet replied, urging her on.

Meanwhile, Milo zeroed in on Rourke by steering his Aktirak right at the gyro-evac. At the last possible second, he jumped from the vehicle and grabbed hold of the netting that covered the balloon. His vehicle, now without a driver, collided with the gyro-evac, tearing a large hole in the side of the balloon.

Below, in the basket, Rourke and Helga felt the gyro-evac dip. "We're losing altitude!" Rourke shouted. "Lighten the load."

Obediently, Helga tossed the last of the fuel tanks overboard. But there was nothing else they could lose.

"That's it," she told Rourke. "Unless someone wants to jump."

Rourke looked around, then shrugged. "Ladies first," he replied. And with a hard shove, he pushed her over the side.

But Helga was not going without a fight. Quick as a cat, she grabbed the side of the basket and in the blink of an eye swung herself back into the cockpit.

"You said we were in this together!" she snarled as

she landed a fierce karate kick squarely in Rourke's stomach. "You promised me a percentage!"

Helga lashed out with another angry kick. But this time Rourke was ready. He caught her foot, twisted it, and tossed her out of the gyro-evac for good.

"Next time, get it in writing," he called as she fell screaming to the bottom of the shaft. "Nothing personal," he added.

In the next second, Rourke felt something on his back—Milo!

"Well, I have to hand it to you," he said as he shrugged Milo off. "You're a bigger pain in the neck than I would have ever thought possible."

With an angry growl and a fierce kick, Rourke sent Milo flying through the railing and out of the balloon. Milo halted his fall by grabbing the chains that held Kida's pod. He began to panic as Rourke climbed down after him, determined to finish him off.

Meanwhile, Helga lay on the ground, barely alive. With her last ounce of strength, she pulled a flare gun out of her holster, aimed it straight at the gyro-evac, and fired! She smiled as the giant balloon burst into flames.

"Nothing personal," she muttered.

Milo and Rourke were so intent on their struggle that they didn't even notice. Rourke had grabbed an ax from the emergency casing and was swinging it wildly at Milo's head. Milo ducked and dodged as the blade swished past his ear—and smashed through the glass window of Kida's pod.

The window shattered into tiny pieces—each one glowing with blue crystal energy. And this gave Milo an idea.

He grabbed a glass shard from the broken window. As Rourke reached out to grab him by the throat, Milo sliced his arm.

Instantly, Rourke's arm—then his whole body—began to crystallize. But this time, the transformation was very different. The Crystal seemed to sense Rourke's evil. Instead of becoming blue as Kida had, Rourke changed to an angry red, then turned black and shiny like a lump of coal.

Milo slumped back against the pod and rubbed his throat. "Thank heaven," he said with a sigh.

But Rourke was not finished yet! With a final surge of energy, he reached for Milo. Milo scrambled away and up the chains, desperate to avoid Rourke's grasp. Slowly, slowly, Rourke pursued Milo, getting closer and closer with every passing second. But when Milo climbed around the balloon's spinning blades to avoid their deadly slicing motion, Rourke did not follow suit. He seemed to be in a trance, as if he were not clearly seeing or feeling the world around him. Unbelievably, Rourke climbed right into the path of the propeller blades—and in an instant, his crystallized form was cracked into a million pieces. Rourke was no more.

A split second later, as the gyro-evac sank closer and closer to the ground, the chains snapped. The princess pod fell, rolled off a sloping rock, and came to a stop at the base of the volcano shaft. Milo gasped. Quickly, with the flaming gyro-evac falling after him, Milo jumped the short distance from the balloon to the ground. His heart in his throat, he sprang into action. With a mighty push, he rolled the princess pod out of harm's way—just in time.

With a loud *KA-BOOOM*, the gyro-evac hit the ground and exploded in an enormous ball of flames.

Almost before Milo could recover from the close call, he had another big problem to deal with. Spidery cracks were spreading across the volcano floor.

"The volcano!" Mole exclaimed as he stared at the ground. "She awakes!"

Sure enough, bright orange lava was welling up through the cracks.

"Hey," quipped Vinny with his hands up, "I had nothing to do with it."

"This here would be a good place not to be," Cookie said.

"No, wait." Milo pointed to Kida. "We gotta get her back or the whole city will die!"

"If we don't get out of here, *we'll* die!" Audrey replied.

But Milo was not giving up. "It's the only way to reverse this," he said as he grabbed a chain. "Just do it!"

Quickly, he hooked one end of the chain to the princess pod and the other to Audrey's Martag. Then he climbed aboard the vehicle. Audrey revved her engine and lifted off, but almost immediately, the chain snapped! The princess pod fell to the ground once again.

Without a moment's hesitation, Milo rappelled down the chain and onto the pod. He wrapped the chain around the pod, and as the lava began to bubble up around him, he held on for dear life.

"Go!" he shouted.

Back inside the city of Atlantis, Milo hurried to pry open the door of Kida's pod.

Using the tip of an Atlantean spear, he had managed to open a corner when the walls of the pod flew apart to reveal the glowing princess. For a moment, she hovered in the air above the pod; then she began to rise, higher and higher, until she was floating hundreds of feet above the central plaza. At the same time, the King Stones were reawakened by Kida's return. With a powerful burst of energy, they rose into the air, where they took their places around Kida.

Mole noticed a thin stream of lava beginning to ooze through a small crack in the cave walls at the edge of the city.

"The fissure—it's about to eject its pyroclastic fury!" Mole exclaimed.

"Milo!" Dr. Sweet translated. "Mole says the wall's gonna blow!"

Milo looked from Kida to the lava and back to the glowing princess. The stones were now spinning around her, and she was becoming brighter and brighter. One by one, the fallen statues Milo had seen throughout Atlantis—the Stone Giants—were coming to life, rising to their feet and forming a ring around the city.

At that moment, to everyone's horror, the cave wall gave way and the now unobstructed lava started to pour through with mad fury. Like a tidal wave, it bore down on Atlantis. Milo held his breath. The entire city was about to be flooded with fiery hot lava.

But just before the wave reached the city, the Stone Giants clapped their hands in one synchronized motion. The mighty clap echoed like thunder, and a protective dome of pure energy spread over Atlantis.

The dome acted like a giant shield, just as it had during the Great Flood. The lava flowed over Atlantis without touching the city itself. For a few moments, it sat cooling and hardening like a shell over the city. Then it crumbled to pieces and harmlessly fell away.

High above Atlantis, Kida had stopped glowing. She was floating down toward Milo, and as she drew closer and closer to him, he could see that her crystalline form was slowly transforming back into flesh. She was returning to her old self!

Thousands of years before, Kida's mother had sacrificed herself for her people after they had used the Crystal's powers for evil purposes. Now Kida had given herself to the Crystal too. But this time, Milo and the Atlanteans had used the Crystal's powers for good. And for that reason, the Crystal was giving Kida back.

"Milo," she whispered as she floated down into his open arms.

She opened her hand to find a tiny gold bracelet. It was the bracelet her mother had taken from Kida's wrist the day they were parted forever.

Kida threw her arms around Milo as her emotions overwhelmed her. Then the steam over the city slowly cleared, and Kida and Milo stood together as a beautiful new Atlantis was revealed. The crumbling ruins and statues were gone, and in their place was a perfect vision of Atlantis as it had been long, long before. But it wasn't a vision—it was real!

# CHAPTER 12

**"A**tlantis will honor your names forever," Kida told the crew of explorers assembled before her. "I only wish there was more we could do for you."

Vinny stared at the Martag being loaded up with gold and jewels and other priceless Atlantean treasures—all for the explorers to take back to the surface with them.

"Ah, you know, thanks anyway. But, eh, I think we're good," he said.

Milo nodded toward the row of Martags. "They'll take you as far as the surface," he said.

There, Milo knew, Mr. Whitmore would be waiting. Within a week, the crew would be home. But Milo would not be with them.

"We're really gonna miss you, Milo," Audrey said, shaking her head.

"Yeah." Vinny nodded. "You know, I'm gonna reopen that flower shop . . . and I'm gonna think of you guys every single day . . . Monday through Friday. Nine to five. Saturday until two. Sunday—I'm gonna take Sunday off, probably, but . . ."

While Vinny rambled on, Cookie stepped up and pulled a small barrel out of his waders.

"I ain't so good at speechifying . . . ," he told Milo, "but I wanted you to have this. It's the bacon grease from the whole trip."

"Cookie . . . I . . ."

But Cookie had already turned away, tears running down into his beard.

Audrey gave Milo a kiss on the cheek, then faked a punch. "Ah-hah! Two for flinching!" she joked, lightly punching his arm. "See ya, Milo!"

Then Mole walked up.

"Ah, Milo!" he said tearfully, reaching out to hug him.

"Mole!" Milo tried to back away. But then the moment overwhelmed him almost as much as Mole's odor, and he held his breath and gave Mole's head a little pat.

"Are you sure you want to stay?" Dr. Sweet asked Milo when it was his turn to say good-bye. "There's a hero's welcome waiting for the man who discovered Atlantis."

Milo shook his head. "I don't think the world needs another hero," he replied. "Besides, I hear there's an opening down here for an expert in gibberish."

Dr. Sweet chuckled and held out his hand. "You take good care of yourself, Milo Thatch," he said.

"Yeah, you too, Sweet," Milo said, shaking the doctor's hand. Dr. Sweet pulled Milo in for a bear hug.

"Can we go home now?" Mrs. Packard called impatiently from across the plaza.

Dr. Sweet rolled his eyes. "C'mon, y'all!" he shouted as he put more film in his camera. "Let's get one last picture in front of the fish!"

# EPILOGUE

**B**ack at his mansion, Preston Whitmore leafed through the photos of the Atlantis expedition.

"Now, let's go over it again," he told the crew assembled in his study, "just so we've got it straight. You didn't find anything."

"Nope," said Vinny, shaking his head. "Just a lot of rocks . . . and fish . . . little fish. Sponges."

The billionaire looked down at a photo of a carved stone flying fish and nodded. He understood that Atlantis must stay hidden from the world. "And what happened to Helga?" he asked.

"Well," Cookie began, "we lost her when the flaming zeppelin come down on her—"

Suddenly Whitmore's umbrella came crashing down on Cookie's head.

"Uh, missing," Cookie corrected himself.

"That's right." Whitmore nodded again. "And Rourke?"

"Nervous breakdown," said Dr. Sweet. "You could say he went all to pieces."

Whitmore's mustache twitched as he tried to hide his smile. "And what about Milo?" he asked finally.

"Went down with the sub," Audrey answered with a sigh.

Mr. Whitmore flipped to a picture of Milo standing next to Kida. "I'm gonna miss that boy," he said. "At least he's in a better place now."

Whitmore held up the crystal pendant Milo had sent back for him and reread the note that Milo had enclosed.

Dear Mr. Whitmore,

I hope this piece of proof
is enough for you. It sure
convinced me. Thanks from
both of us.

Milo

Then Mr. Whitmore smiled as he placed the glowing crystal around his neck.

As far as the rest of the world was concerned, their expedition to Atlantis had been a complete failure. But for Mr. Whitmore and the crew of the *Ulysses,* it was the most successful voyage ever.

Meanwhile, thousands of leagues beneath the ocean, Milo was indeed in a far better place. He was in Atlantis with someone he loved.

Together, he and Kida put the finishing touches on a new King Stone—one with a long white beard and tattoos across its nose and forehead. Then, as she wiped away a tear, the new queen kissed her crystal pendant and touched it to the statue. That was all it took. In an instant, the statue of her father rose into the air. And as the citizens of Atlantis looked on, the majestic stone took its place in orbit around the Crystal.

And that was where it would stay, if Kida and Milo had their way, until the end of time.